CHRIS MAKES A FRIEND

ALEX GINO

Scholastic Press / New York

Copyright © 2025 by Alex Gino

All rights reserved. Published by Scholastic Press, an imprint of Scholastic Inc., *Publishers since 1920.* SCHOLASTIC, SCHOLASTIC PRESS, and associated logos are trademarks and/or registered trademarks of Scholastic Inc.

The publisher does not have any control over and does not assume any responsibility for author or third-party websites or their content.

No part of this publication may be reproduced, stored in a retrieval system, or transmitted in any form or by any means, electronic, mechanical, photocopying, recording, or otherwise, or used to train any artificial intelligence technologies, without written permission of the publisher. For information regarding permission, write to Scholastic Inc., Attention: Permissions Department, 557 Broadway, New York, NY 10012.

This book is a work of fiction. Names, characters, places, and incidents are either the product of the author's imagination or are used fictitiously, and any resemblance to actual persons, living or dead, business establishments, events, or locales is entirely coincidental.

Library of Congress Cataloging-in-Publication Data available

ISBN 978-1-5461-3817-4

10 9 8 7 6 5 4 3 2 1   25 26 27 28 29

Printed in Italy   208
First edition, November 2025

Book design by Maeve Norton

*To my little sister Robin,
someone I never ever ever ever thought
I would dedicate a book to.*

PART I

CHAPTER 1

Mom and Frank picked us up from school for the last time ever. Well, Becca would be back to the elementary school for third grade in September, but I was headed to middle school for sixth grade, so this was the last time for me anyway. I was in the car the moment it pulled up. Mom had to call three times before Becca finally finished hugging her entire friend group, one by one.

Frank had been driving us home from school by herself lately, but since this was the last day, it was the Official First Ice Cream Trip of the Summer. Mom said not even chronic pain could keep her from that tradition.

Chronic pain means pain that doesn't go away with time. Mom's neck and back always hurt, at least a little bit. She even printed out a meme and posted it on the fridge that said:

I have chronic pain.
If I don't say it hurts, it hurts.
If I say it hurts, it hurts A LOT.

For Mom, a good day meant that she could get up and drive us to school and go to work and do the normal things she did, but by the end of the day, she was in bed with a heating pad, and if I wanted to watch TV with her, we had to do it in her room. But that was a *good* day, and Mom hadn't really had a good day in a while. She had to stop going to work about two months ago, and more often than not, her bedroom door was closed and she'd be taking a nap when we got home in the afternoon.

Frank didn't officially live with us as Mom's girlfriend, but she'd been staying over a lot lately, especially on weeknights, to help us all get ready in the morning. I thought she was pretty great, and she said that we had lots in common, even though she was a nonbinary butch and I was pretty sure I was a cisgender girl. For example, we both loved videos of bunnies nibbling on carrots and neither of us liked being called the long versions of our names.

"Chris, you're on my side!" Becca screamed, just because my middle finger crossed the piece of masking tape Mom had run down the center of the back seat to keep us from fighting. It was only the tip, and it was only for a second. She wasn't even using that part of the seat. And besides, my body was bigger than hers, so really, it wasn't fair that she got as much of the middle as I did.

"Your stuff was all over my side yesterday and I didn't say anything," I pointed out. She'd been making paper airplanes, and lots of her papers had had at least one corner on my side of the tape, if not two.

"You two are lucky I didn't have a third child," Mom said sharply, "because then you wouldn't have any of that middle seat to fight about."

"It's the last day of school," Frank noted with a sigh. "You'd think that would be enough to keep them from fighting. Not to mention ice cream!"

"My kids have talents beyond words."

Mom and Frank laughed, though I don't know how much they were laughing at what Mom said versus how much they were laughing at us.

Frank pulled into Udder Delights, the fancy ice cream shop that made all their own flavors. Becca and I ran up to a line long enough that it stretched out of the shop and past the nail salon next door. Frank joined us a minute later.

"Where's Mommy?" Becca asked.

"Right over there." Frank gestured to the small round tables with wire metal seats, painted white and shaded by large red-and-white-striped umbrellas. I always felt so elegant in those chairs, like we were sitting by the Seine River in Paris. I spotted Mom, with her foam neck brace and the special cushion she used for her back. She gave me a broad smile, but when I looked again, it had faded into nervousness.

A family with a little kid joined the line, and Becca gave them a huge wave. The kid waved back shyly.

"Who's that?" Frank asked.

"Oh, that's JR. He goes to kindergarten at our school. Or at least he used to. He'll be in first grade next year. I hope he gets Ms. Clemens. Then he'll have frogs in his classroom and he might get to take them home one weekend."

I had never seen that kid before in my life. I didn't even know Ms. Clemens's class had frogs.

The line moved quickly and soon we were ordering. Once we had our ice cream—cups for Becca and me and cones for Mom and Frank—we joined Mom outside. The air was warm, but the shade of the umbrella protected us from the worst of the heat.

I took a bite of my maple scoop. Maple might sound like a boring ice cream flavor, but it's so creamy and delicious and there are crystallized bits of maple syrup to crunch on. And under that was a scoop of Brownie Dream, because chocolate is life.

By the time Mom laid it on us, my guard was totally down.

"I'm sure you've noticed that my neck's been a little worse lately." She rocked her head side to side against her brace as she said it, like bringing it up reminded her that she wasn't in a comfortable position, and she kept going, even though moving reminded her that *none* of the positions were comfortable. "I've talked with my doctor, and I really need to take it seriously."

Frank nodded in agreement. I didn't even know what was up yet but I knew I didn't like it.

"You know I love you both, right?" Mom said.

Becca nodded, her eyes open with fear. Mine were narrowed.

"Just rip off the Band-Aid, Mom!" I said.

Frank chuckled, but nervously, like she knew she wasn't really supposed to.

"Okay, okay," said Mom. "So the heart of it is, I'm going to be having surgery next week."

"Surgery?" I yelled.

"Next week?" Becca yelled.

"I know it's a lot." Mom spoke so calmly it made me nervous. "And I know it's sudden. But something is shifting in my neck and the doctor wants to get in there as soon as possible."

"Will you be okay?" Becca asked.

"As okay as I can be," answered Mom, which really wasn't much of an answer.

"The doctors said the success rate on this surgery is pretty high," Frank reassured us.

"That's good?" Becca asked.

Mom laughed. "That's very good. Most people who have the surgery feel much better within a few months, and very few people say it didn't help at all."

"How long will you be in the hospital?" I asked. Mom had gotten surgery a couple of years ago. Becca was too young to remember it, but it took a week for Mom to come home, and Dad's parents had visited from Florida to help take care of us. Dad still lived with us then.

"Well, the doctor said three to five days, but even once I get back home, I'm going to be on strict bed rest."

"Even more than now?" asked Becca. I had to admit she had a point. Mom was in bed most of the day, even for meals. She had a special mechanical bed so she could raise the top half and sit up, but she was in too much pain to sit at the table most days, or even on the couch.

"Even more than now," Mom confirmed. "Full-out lying down with as few distractions as possible. I love you both, but you *can* be distracting, to say the least. Sooo"—Mom drew out the word, and I could feel my peaceful summer of reading on the couch slip out of my grasp—"I've arranged a little vacation for the two of you."

"You're going to send us away?" I asked. If Mom was going to have surgery, I understood that she shouldn't have to deal with Becca's noise. But it hurt to think I was more trouble than help.

"We can be good!" Becca said, her eyes wet.

"It's not like I'm sending you off with strangers," Mom said to me sternly, then softened as she turned to Becca. "You are very good, and you do a great job when I need to rest. But you do still need to eat."

"Chris can make us food!"

"No, I can't!" I wasn't sure whose side I was on. Too much was happening all at once. "What about Frank?"

"You need to be with an adult who can be on top of things, and this summer that's not going to be me. I'm going to be focused on this one." Frank pointed at Mom.

"Wait—summer?" I asked. "How long is this *little vacation* going to be?"

"Well, when we started talking about it, the doctor said even a week or two would be helpful."

"Two whole weeks!" Becca cried.

"It's about to get worse," I warned her. Adults liked to slow play kids like this, starting with the smallest version of something that was about to get huge. And if two weeks was the small version, summer was about to be destroyed.

"Is it?" Becca looked at Mom with giant eyes.

"Well, I wouldn't say *worse*," Mom said. "But your sister's right. It's going be longer than two weeks. All told, the doctor recommended that if I can get eight weeks of uninterrupted healing time, that would be best."

"Eight weeks!" Becca yelled. "That's an octopus's worth!"

"It's also two months," I said, translating into a time unit more comprehensible than cephalopod limbs. Practically the entire summer.

"Frank and I talked about it, and we decided that six weeks would be a good balance." Mom gave a weak smile.

It seemed to me that balance should have included asking your children how they felt. I took a bite of my ice cream but couldn't really taste it, not even the chocolate.

"Besides, that's about as long as Nana and Papa would have you," Mom joked, trying to soften the situation.

"Nana and Papa?!" Becca and I exclaimed at once.

We'd visited them plenty of times before, but always with Mom. They were nice enough, but they believed that a kid indoors on a summer afternoon was a terrible thing, even if that kid was curled up in a comfortable chair, happily reading a great book. Even if they were inside themselves.

"Not Nonny and Pops?" asked Becca. "They have a pool!" A summer with Nonny and Pops would have meant a summer of lounging on the couch in air-conditioning with my tablet in one hand and a book in the other.

Mom shook her head, then winced. "When am I going to remember to stop doing that?" she asked herself, then addressed Becca. "Going down to Nonny and Pops would mean a flight down to Florida and another flight back for whoever took you. Massachusetts is just a few hours drive."

Mom didn't mention that visiting Nonny and Pops also meant thinking about Dad, a man Mom referred to as "your father, who I will not speak ill of to your face"... which was a polite way of saying she hated his guts.

Nana and Papa lived past the middle of nowhere, in Western Massachusetts, and all their neighbors were trees. In the summer, when those trees were full of leaves, you couldn't see the next house in any direction. That meant there weren't any neighborhood kids that Nana and Papa would tell me to spend time with, but that also meant there weren't any neighborhood kids for Becca to play with instead of bothering me. At least I'd have plenty of time to read, even if I had to read every book outdoors.

"So when are you driving us to Old People Summer Camp?" I asked Frank.

"Saturday."

Saturday?

Saturday!

It was already Tuesday afternoon. I needed to cram six weeks' worth of fun with my best friend Vicky into three days, not to mention pack, and also snuggle Mom until she said I was a squirmy bug and she needed to rest.

"You're coming too, right, Mommy?" asked Becca.

Mom made a face where the corner of her lip jerked down and away from the rest of her face like it was trying to run away from an awkward moment.

"You're not even coming to see your parents before you have surgery?!" I felt bad about yelling. Sort of. It wasn't Mom's fault that her neck was all messed up.

"Wait," said Becca, her face dripping like her ice cream cone. "You're not driving us?"

"No, she's not," I said. "She can't drive, remember?" I turned to Mom. "But you're not even gonna ride in the passenger's seat?"

Frank answered for her. "Your mom and I talked about it, and the drive is real hard on her body. It's going to be best this time around for me to drive you myself."

"I hate that!" Becca pouted.

"Yeah," I added. "Ouch."

My words were flat, but the hurt in Becca's voice matched the hurt in my heart. It was rare that Becca and I had the same reaction to anything.

Mom didn't even point out that I had just agreed with my sister, which meant that she had to be in a lot of pain. Another wave of feeling bad passed over me when I realized that.

"So Frank will be driving you up," Mom said, and I could tell it was meant to end the discussion.

Becca didn't take the hint.

"And you will be driving us back down when you come and get us?" she asked.

"I'm not sure, sweetie," said Mom. "I want to, but we'll see how I do with surgery and a little rest."

"The whole summer is not a *little* rest," I mutter.

"It's not the whole summer," Mom said.

"It's an awful lot of it."

"I know," said Mom, and the sadness in her voice made me feel bad that I was mad at her. But that didn't mean I wasn't.

"Wait!" Becca yelled, and I could practically see the gears turning in her tiny mind. "If we're not here, how am I gonna see Lizette and Emily and Maisha and Rachel and Erin? And how can we practice our soccer moves together?" Her face got all wrinkly and ready to cry again.

That was just like Becca, turning Mom's surgery into a problem about her not seeing her bazillions of friends.

"Don't worry," I said. "I'm sure the flowers in Papa's garden will be happy to be your friends."

"You don't get it!" she shot back. "You don't have friends!"

"That's enough," Frank said firmly. "Your mom has a few tough weeks ahead of her and you fighting doesn't make it any easier. We all need to help, okay? And your way of helping is going to visit Nana and Papa. Do you understand?"

We both nodded.

"Why don't you two tell us about your last day of school?" said Mom, trying to distract us. "I know it's a big deal, moving up to third grade."

Becca was foolish enough to fall for this, and soon we were listening to how the second-grade teacher let them wash the desks and the blackboard and everything, as if cleaning was some sort of privilege.

"Now if you could only clean up your room at home!" Mom joked.

I was the only one who didn't laugh. The rest of them could switch onto another topic, but I was determined to stay sour about the trip, even if it ruined the First Ice Cream Trip of the Summer.

Which, if I'm being completely honest, it did.

CHAPTER 2

"I hereby call the first meeting of the Great Summer 72 Book Challenge, henceforth to be known as GS72BC, to order," declared Vicky, banging her pencil against the table as if she were holding a judge's gavel.

We were sitting on the floor around the coffee table in her living room, which was dusted and tidy—two words that were never used to describe *my* family's living room. We had each brought ten books we were excited to read and ten books we had already read and wanted to share. Or at least that had been the plan. We each had more like twenty books we wanted to read, and more like two or three to hand off because we'd already given each other our favorite books back when we'd first read them and couldn't stop gushing about them. The rest of the table was taken up with matching purple sparkle notebooks to log our progress, a bag of potato chips, and two glasses of lemonade.

We came up with the idea of GS72BC because of all the books we wanted to read that summer. There were seventy-two days of school break, so we set a great big goal to each read a book a day: the Great Summer 72 Book Challenge. We planned to meet up as many afternoons as possible to read and eat snacks together.

Now everything had changed. I wasn't sure how I was going to tell Vicky that our plans were going to be a little different than expected.

"Roll call!" I announced. It was silly, since it was just Vicky and me, but it gave me a few more seconds before the meeting really started. "Vicky Chan?"

"Here!" Vicky raised her hand dutifully.

"Chris Rossi?" I called, then answered myself in my fanciest voice, "Present."

"Great," said Vicky. "That's everyone. This meeting is officially convened."

She looked at me. I looked at her. She kept looking at me. I kept looking at her. Did she already know? Had my mom told her mom or something?

"Vicky—" I started, but she cut me off.

"Wait, before you say anything, I have something to tell you. Don't be mad at me."

"Why would I be mad at you?" I thought she couldn't possibly have news as bad as mine.

Vicky wrinkled her face. "Well, it turns out I may be busy from noon to five some days this summer."

"That's prime reading time!" I was aware I was being hypocritical. Vicky's news was like a beautiful birdsong in comparison with mine. My news was a waterlogged tuba played by a fox with a breathing problem. My tuba made her birdsong irrelevant. Still, I wasn't ready to tell her *my* news, so I asked, "Why? What happened?"

"My parents signed me up for a thing."

"What kind of thing?"

"Some theater camp." Vicky shrugged. "She said it would help me be a little less shy around new people."

"New people are the worst!" I scrunched my face into a ball of disdain.

"I know," said Vicky, "but maybe these people won't be too bad. I mean, theater kids are supposed to be cool and stuff."

"Forget what I said. New people *who are cool* are the worst." I side-eyed Vicky. I was acting like I was mad at her news, which really wasn't fair, when really I was mad at my own news. News I hadn't even told her yet.

"I don't mean like school cool," Vicky floundered. "I mean like laid-back weirdos."

"So, like, the opposite of cool."

"Maybe. But they're not *you*. I wish you could come."

"I can't."

"Yeah, it's expensive." Vicky's parents both had jobs that paid well. Mom called it a two-income household, and it meant that they had more money to pool together for things like camp.

"No, I mean, I can't." As much as I wished it wasn't, my problem was still there, front and center, and now that I had found my opening, I knew I couldn't back away, or I'd never say it and Vicky would be waiting for me on her couch and I would already be in Massachusetts. "I . . . well . . . your camp may really not matter all that much. I mean, for GS72BC. I won't be here for the next six weeks."

Vicky's face froze, her mouth open well before she spoke. "Wait, are you super sick?"

"No!" At least my news wasn't as bad as that.

Vicky's body relaxed. "Sorry. I just read a book where the best friend dies and it was the worst."

"Yeah, that's totally a thing in books and I hate it. But no, I'm fine."

"So, what is it?" Vicky asked, a nervous shake still in her voice.

"Well, you know how my mom has problems with her neck, right?"

"Yeahhh?" Vicky's eyes asked, *And what does that have to do with anything?*

"Well, she's having surgery next week."

"Oh," said Vicky. "Is she gonna be okay?"

"Yeah, it's gonna help with her pain a lot, but first she has to recover, and that means that it needs to be quiet at home. So . . ." I wish I didn't have to say it. Saying things made them feel realer. "Becca and I are going to stay with my grandparents in Massachusetts."

"For six weeks?"

I nodded.

Vicky's face brightened. "That's how long the theater

camp is too. We'll still have almost a month when you get back."

"Optimist," I said, like it was an insult. Sometimes I loved the way Vicky looked at the bright side of things, but other times I just wanted her to be annoyed at the world along with me.

"Hey, I thought you had some strange unnamed illness or something, so I'm super glad it's not that."

"Still, six weeks is like forever. Especially in summer, when the days are mega long. And, like, I get Mom and Frank not wanting Becca and all her noise around, but I'm a pretty quiet kid."

"I've seen you yell," said Vicky.

"Yeah, if Becca's bothering me. But if it's just Mom and Frank and me, I don't see what the problem is. Becca could go by herself and I could stay here."

"Good luck telling your mom that."

"Yeah, no, I'm not even trying. It just sucks."

"It sure does." Vicky sighed.

I met her sigh with an even bigger sigh, which she matched with a truly huge sigh. We went back and forth with that, expressing our exasperation, until Vicky dramatically flopped her body flat to the ground and rolled around in mock agony, complete with moans and whimpers.

"Maybe you'll be good at theater camp after all." I tried to smile.

"Thanks." Vicky sat back up and we stared at the floor in the sad quiet for a bit.

"What about GS72BC?" Vicky said it first, but it was already in the air. And I wish I had said it first, because her asking made it seem like I was supposed to have some sort of answer, and I most certainly did not.

"I mean, we're still doing it, right?" I asked.

"Of course!" said Vicky. "It's just gonna be way less fun if we aren't sitting around reading together."

"True."

"Are you still going to have time to read in Massachusetts?"

"Are you kidding me? My grandparents are big on making sure we don't get too much screen time. I'm going to have nothing but time to read. The real question is: Are you still going to have time if you're at camp?"

"It won't be every day. I think it might only be Tuesdays and Thursdays. And I can probably read while I'm there too. I'm sure there'll be plenty of times I'll be bored. And we can always check in when we video call."

It wasn't all that bad that I was going to be away, I tried to tell myself. We had already decided to skip weekends because of family barbecues and getaways and stuff, plus we were going to miss another two days a week for Vicky's camp.

GS72BC was still on. Plus, I'd get to spend so much time by myself, reading without anyone interrupting me. Vicky talked a lot about how much fun it was to read together, but if I was telling the real truth, I'd have admitted it was also kind of nice to be the only person around and not have to think about anything but you and your book. Nobody else's breathing or chewing. Nobody else's shifting around and knocking into your elbow. Not even anybody else's exclaiming about an exciting moment in a book you gave them to read, which sounds like fun except when you're in the middle of the sequel and you keep getting interrupted by someone who wants to gossip about what was going on with the main character way back in the beginning of the first book, before she learned about her superpowers.

"Well, it seems you won the bad news game," Vicky offered. "Even if you're not, like, dying."

"What's my prize?" I asked.

"You get to pick the first book I read." Vicky beamed.

"In that case . . ." I pulled out *Swords & Secrets*, the first Magical Mysterious Vidalia book. It was the best book I'd read all year, maybe ever. I kept trying to make references to the world of Vidalia, but Vicky never got any of them. And no matter how many times I begged her to read it, she always said she would get to it next and never did.

"Why am I not surprised?"

"I know you don't usually like fantasy books, but Vidalia is special." I tossed the book into her lap. Vicky acted like the 400-page hardcover was as heavy as a hippo. She flailed as if she were being crushed under its weight.

"I promise it'll go fast," I said.

"Aren't there three of them?" Vicky eyed me skeptically.

"If you don't want to read the other two after you finish this, that's on you. So, what am *I* reading?"

Vicky handed me a soft blue book from my own pile with a girl's face on the cover, sailboats reflected in her eyes. She held her hands out, touching her index and thumb fingers. From this, along with the title, *Show Me a Sign*, I guessed that the girl was Deaf. Vicky had lent it to me months ago, but there was always something else I needed to read first.

"Is there any other business to cover before we read?" Vicky asked.

"You mean other than the fact that you had bad news and I had worse news?" I asked.

"I'm hoping it's not *all* bad. At least, not camp. You won't be there, but the website actually looked kind of cool."

"And my news?" I asked.

"Okay, your news is pretty terrible," Vicky admitted.

"See, all I was saying was my news was worse." I cheesed a grin. "You already said so."

"Well," said Vicky, "if there's nothing else, I say we get started."

I set an alarm for forty-five minutes on my tablet. Frank was coming to pick me up in an hour and we needed at least a few minutes to hug and say goodbye a thousand times before that. We opened our books and the room went quiet, other than the sounds of munching on potato chips and the occasional laugh or gasp.

"How have I not already read this?" I asked when the alarm beeped. "It's historical fiction, but it reads like a regular modern book."

Vicky shrugged.

"No, how have you not already put this into my hands?" I asked. "You should have told me it was going to be this good."

"I did." Vicky laughed. "The whole time I read it, I kept thinking how much you would love it. Just wait until it really gets going."

"Sometimes I think you know me better than I know me," I said.

"Sometimes maybe that's what a best friend is. I'm gonna miss you this summer."

"It's not like I'm gonna go off and make a new best friend."

"You'd better not!" Vicky said.

"I won't!" I assured her. "Don't you go making a new best friend either."

"Unlikely."

Unless Becca and I were about to become best friends, it was just going to be a summer of me, my books, and the cozy chair on Nana and Papa's porch where I usually spend most of my visits. I'd miss Vicky and Mom, of course, and Frank too, but I'd be fine alone with my books.

CHAPTER 3

Frank arrived on Saturday morning with two cups of ice coffee, a bag of bagels, and two tubs of cream cheese—plain for me and scallion for Mom and her. I liked sesame seed bagels toasted and covered in cream cheese. Becca ate her plain bagels cold and dry.

"Better enjoy 'em while you can," Frank said. "They don't have decent bagels in Massachusetts."

"They don't?" I brought one of the coffees to Mom. She was sitting in her bed, heating pack on her back and ice pack on her neck.

"You get great cider donuts in fall," Mom offered.

"We're not going to be there in the fall!" I put Mom's special long straw into the coffee and gave it to her. Even lifting the cup to her mouth hurt these days.

"Relax," said Mom. She took a sip of coffee and let the straw fall to the side. "I'm just saying every place has something special about it, and I'm sure you'll find some local treats. The side-of-the-road ice cream places are fantastic."

I didn't smile, but I did let my face soften up a bit.

Back in the kitchen, Frank brought the cutting board and a large bread knife to the table, and cut bagels in half for herself, Mom, and me. I know how to use a knife, but it's kind of hard to get an even cut on a bagel. Mom can't really cut a bagel either these days. She doesn't hold the knife with her neck or anything, but she has to use lots of muscles to cut. Frank even spread the cream cheese for her. I spread my own cream cheese.

"Becca must not have heard me come in," said Frank, once we were settled in Mom's bed with our bagels. "Why don't you go ask your sister to join us?"

I groaned. I didn't really *talk* to my sister. I'd talk to Mom and Becca would hear, or Becca would talk to Mom and I'd hear, or Mom would ask us a question and we'd answer separately. But I can't remember the last time I voluntarily said something directly to Becca when we weren't also talking with other people. I yelled at her sometimes, sure, but there wasn't really anything I wanted her to know except to leave me alone. And there certainly weren't any questions I needed her answer to . . . except maybe if she'd ever leave me alone.

"Is there a problem?" Mom raised an eyebrow.

"Do I have to? Can't we just sit here quietly and tell Becca the bagels are here once we're done eating? Or at least, once I'm done eating?"

"Because?" Frank asked, like she genuinely didn't know. Or if she did, she was hiding it well.

"Because she's the most annoying person in the entire universe!"

"You're exaggerating," said Mom.

"She's right," added Frank. "We don't have data on most of the universe."

"Okay, fine. The most annoying person on the planet!"

That's when Mom started talking about how Becca just wants to spend time with me because she loves me and looks up to me and all that big sibling stuff.

This went on a while, until Mom concluded, "In the

grand scheme of your life, the annoyance you feel now is insignificant to the amount she'll mean to you someday."

Which about made me want to vomit. I even made a few retching sounds.

"Significance is relative." Frank gave her usual smile that either said she had no idea the trouble she was causing, or maybe she knew entirely the trouble she was causing. And her even tone did nothing to tip the scales. "I mean, how many times have you freaked out because you woke up late? Twenty minutes is an insignificant part of your life, but how often do we look at life all at once?"

Now it was Mom who groaned. "Do you have to be this deep at breakfast?"

"24-7-365.24!" This time Frank's smile said that she either enjoyed bothering Mom or being exact about the length of the average year.

"If you keep this up, there's no way you'll get out of here on time," said Mom.

"Yeah, but will we be *significantly* late?" I asked, making

Mom and Frank both laugh so hard they forgot they had asked me to get Becca.

I was going to miss being goofy with Mom and Frank like this.

We did not leave on time.

Frank was still upstairs with Mom forty-five minutes after we were supposed to leave. Everything, even getting dressed, took longer for Mom because of her chronic pain. And while her friends were coming over soon to spend the day, Mom felt more comfortable getting help from Frank for things like washing up.

I was on the three steps that led to the front door of our building, reading about Josephine Baker in *Rad Women Worldwide*. She was an African American performer who became famous in France and was a World War II spy. I wished I was the kind of person who could read in the car without feeling insta-sick. Instead, I crammed in as many pages as I could before we had to get in the car.

Becca practiced cartwheels on the sidewalk, not even realizing how lucky she was to be wearing shorts.

She wasn't very good, but I didn't say anything. I couldn't do a cartwheel at all. I maxed out at a slo-mo tumblesault.

Next to me were two wheelie bags filled with clothes and two duffel bags. Becca's duffel was stuffed with toys and coloring books and things like that. And next to it, of course, was her soccer ball. She had gotten it for her birthday, and since Mom had dropped the news, she had been talking about how she was going to get to practice outside every day. At home, she had to wait for someone to take her to the park, because our apartment building was too small to have a playground.

My duffel had ten books (Mom said I couldn't take more, but she promised that someone would take me to the library as often as I needed and that no one would judge my choices), my tablet charger (my tablet was in my pocket), Becca's tablet (Becca forgot to pack it, so Mom made me take it even though it wasn't really my responsibility), Hoppy (my stuffed bunny, who also happened to make a really good pillow), and that was about it.

"When are we going?" Becca whined at me, as if there was some reason I should have the answer.

"I don't know. When Frank's ready. Don't rush her. The sooner we're in the car, the sooner we have to listen to Nana and Papa telling us to go outside and get some fresh air. And watch for glass on the sidewalk. You don't want to cut your hands."

"I know that. I already checked." But she examined the sidewalk carefully before attempting another gymnastics routine. Then another. And another.

"Look what I can do!" Becca said when Frank finally appeared at the front door. Becca threw her feet over her head, her legs bent and wiggling like a frog.

"Good job! Now run upstairs and use the bathroom one more time before we hit the road. You too, Chris."

"But I just went before I came downstairs."

"Please. I told your mother I would send you both up. Besides, it's the last time you'll see her for a bit."

"More than a bit," I muttered as I plodded after Becca, who had already sprinted toward the door. It's not that I didn't want to hug Mom goodbye. It was more that I hated that we were going at all.

Becca picked up three more toys while we were upstairs and screamed that she couldn't find her tablet until I reminded her that it was already in my bag.

I gave Mom a hug with as much of a squeeze as I dared without hurting her. She couldn't put her arms up to hug me back, so I cuddled in closer to make up for it.

"This is your last summer before middle school. Enjoy it. You'll never be this young again." Mom sounded like she was talking about a memory, even though it hadn't happened yet.

"Isn't that always true for everyone?" I asked.

"Fair." Mom chuckled. "But this is one of those special times. I'm sorry I'm going to miss it in person, but I promise we'll be talking all the time." Mom paused in that way that said she was thinking, not finished, and not to interrupt her. "Alright," she started up again. "I know you aren't your sister's biggest fan."

Understatement.

"But you're in it together this summer. Be gentle on her, okay? And I know you hate when I say this, but remember that you're Becca's big sister, and she looks up to you. You're old enough to have a little more perspective on things than she does."

I do hate it when she says that.

I pressed my side against hers. "So I'm supposed to enjoy being young while also being older?"

Mom paused, then grinned deviously. "Guess so. Life is a weird game and balance is rule number one."

I gave Mom another giant yet delicate hug and let Becca have her turn saying one last goodbye. Becca already had tears on her face and she started sobbing the moment she put her arms around Mom. Mom put a hand on Becca's back to comfort her, and I could tell it hurt because she winced. I hoped the surgery meant that Mom could hug us normally again.

Back downstairs, Frank asked me to put Becca's latest additions to our trip into my bag, since hers was already too full to close. I sighed but packed them in. Then Becca complained that she wanted her tablet in the car, so I had to go through my bag and take a bunch of stuff out to find it. I gave her my earbuds too. Frank said that was kind, but really I did it so we wouldn't have to listen to Becca's videos the whole time. Between her videos and Frank's music, I wouldn't have been able to hear my own music anyway without playing it so loud that it blew out my ears.

I repacked while Frank went down the block and came back with the car. We loaded up, Frank put on her favorite '80s playlist, skipped to a track she said she knew every word of, and proceeded to prove it at the top of her lungs as we hit the road.

We crossed the bridge from Staten Island into New Jersey, part of a herd of vehicles leaving the city while another herd on our left made its way in. If you looked on a map, you might not have thought that a trip from New York to Massachusetts would start off by going west to Jersey, but it was better to go a few extra miles and miss the worst of the city traffic. So we went westward in order to go northeast.

Frank hummed along happily with the music, and sometimes she'd belt out a chorus. Becca was deep in her soccer videos, watching athletes do athletic things with a black-and-white sphere. They all looked the same to me—people running around on grass—but she could watch them for hours. She didn't even watch real games with scores or winners or anything. She just watched people practicing drills.

For the zillionth time, I wished I could look at a book or a screen for more than a minute without wanting to lose my lunch. Instead, I stared out the window at giant building after giant building on either side of the road—warehouses and office parks and factories until more and more trees started to fill in the spaces between the buildings, and the buildings clustered together and then gave way entirely to the trees, broken up by the occasional blip of a town.

The lack of conversation in the car turned from peaceful to stifling as we made our way up the Turnpike. No one had said anything since Frank had pointed out the Manhattan skyline on our right and talked about how the Twin Towers had been at the base of the skyline when she was growing up, and how it was still a little weird not to see them there.

I both wanted the silence to break and didn't want to

be the one to do it. I checked the clock on the car radio, and dared myself not to look again until the minute changed. I failed. Still 10:31. I tried again, waiting, waiting, and success, 10:32. I counted as slowly as I could bear, and by the time I looked again, it was 10:33. I felt like a master of time. And then, this master of time must have fallen asleep because the next thing I realized, we were pulling off the highway.

"Are we almost there?" I asked.

"More like halfway," said Frank. "We're picking up some gas in New Haven."

I looked out the window and registered that we were pulling up to a gas station.

"New York was super short!" said Becca. "Like, not even two episodes long!" Her favorite cartoon, about a family of overly cheerful bears who somehow live in a tree with furniture, was playing on her tablet.

"I know." We'd done this trip before, and there were about twenty-five miles that you spent back in New York before you got to Connecticut. Last year, Becca and I had been fighting and Mom had bet us that we couldn't stay silent through all of New York. She owed us ice cream sundaes for that one, but I had a feeling she didn't really mind losing.

Frank sent us to use the bathroom while she filled up the tank. I didn't have to go, but Becca did, so I had to take her. I tried to tell Frank I could watch the gas pump and she could take Becca in, but she was not convinced.

"You slept through all of New York!" Becca said for the fifth time as we were walking back to the car.

"Yeah, I know."

"And I stayed awake!" Becca bragged.

"Do you want a medal or something?" I asked.

"Don't tease your sister," Frank scolded half-heartedly. We got back in the car and Frank tried to start up a conversation as she pulled back onto the highway. "So, what are you looking forward to at your Nana and Papa's?"

"When it rains so we're allowed to stay inside," I said.

"Really? That's all you've got?" Frank sneaked a look at me in the rearview mirror. "What about you, Becca? Looking forward to a chance to practice your soccer moves? Your Nana and Papa have a huge backyard to run around in."

"Yeah, I'm gonna practice my stepovers and chops."

"See, Chris? It'll be fun."

I failed to see how Becca practicing soccer moves would be fun for me, but Frank continued undeterred. "And your Nana and Papa are both great cooks. You'll eat better than you do at home."

I asked Becca for my earbuds back while she rattled off various soccer drills she was going to practice this summer, with names like toe-taps and cone dribbling. I couldn't watch videos without feeling queasy, but I could listen to music as the trees whirred by, and I did until Becca fell asleep and I switched over to an audiobook.

The Magical Mysterious Vidalia recordings had a full cast, and I already knew the story so I didn't have to worry about missing anything important if Frank needed to belt out a chorus. And Vicky and I had already decided that re-reads of books counted, so I was making progress on GS72BC.

Without Becca talking and fidgeting, things were finally peaceful in the back seat—except, of course, in the land of Vidalia. Ten chapters and thousands of trees later, including Gwenella's trek across the Sulfurous Sands and back, we were in Leverett, Massachusetts.

Leverett was a town so small it was literally just a post office next to a town hall, with a church across the street. There wasn't even a stop sign, and the houses weren't any closer together there than they were along the rest of the county route we'd been driving on. Calling it a town was an insult to real towns. And Nana and Papa's house was still eight minutes away, according to the GPS.

Frank drove down the winding road and then turned onto an even more winding road. Seven million curves later, we were pulling up in front of Nana and Papa's white house with green trim, and my stomach was glad the car had finally stopped moving.

A porch with four large, green rocking chairs ran along the length of the house and, in front of that, a bed of wildflowers. Yellows, reds, pinks, and purples, and Papa knew the names of all of them. I could point out the black-eyed Susans when they bloomed, and I knew that there were hyacinths, because I thought it was a cool name, but I could never remember which ones they were.

Frank hadn't even turned off the engine before Papa was out on the porch.

"Chris, Becca, so good to see my grandkids! Come on up here and give your Papa a big ol' squeeze!" He held his arms out wide for a three-way hug. "And Frank! Good to see you again! How's my daughter?"

"Oh, you know." Frank sighed. "She's been better. But I think this summer is gonna be just what she needs. Thank you for watching the kids."

"Oh, you don't need to thank us for taking care of our grandchildren," said Nana, who I hadn't even noticed join us on the porch. She dried her hands on her red gingham apron before hugging and kissing each of us in turn, even Frank.

"Have you had lunch?" Nana asked Frank.

"Not yet," said Frank. "But I do want to get back home. I'll pick up something on the way."

"You gotta eat!" said Papa. "It's already past lunchtime.

And no offense to the Golden Arches, but my wife's meatballs are pretty spectacular."

"He's not wrong!" Nana winked and opened the front door. An unmistakable whiff of tomato sauce lit up my eyes. Nana had made meatballs and sauce, and Papa was right—Nana's meatballs were amazing. Not even Mom's were as good, and she swore she did everything Nana did.

Frank must have smelled the sauce too, because a smile grew on her face as she said, "I'm sure your daughter would want me to enjoy your cooking."

Frank, Nana, and Papa spent most of lunch talking about Mom, and how they hoped the surgery was going to help. Apparently, sometimes after neck surgery, the person didn't even feel better. And if they did feel better, it could take up to a year to get there.

No one asked what I thought about any of it, which was fine by me, because it meant I could finish eating early and sneak a little time on my tablet before Frank left and our electronics were whisked off to summer jail with limited visiting hours.

Mom says it's good to have some discipline around

screen time, and she wishes she had the energy to be more diligent in setting limits for us. But it seems silly to do it in summer when we don't have any homework.

Last summer when we visited, I'd asked for my tablet for just one minute after lunch, and instead I got a lecture from Nana about how those weird screen lights couldn't possibly be good for my vision. Then she said that when she'd complained of being bored as a child, her grandmother had made her count grains of rice. I hadn't even said I was bored. I'd just wanted to look up something that Papa had said at lunch that I wasn't sure was true. It turned out it he was right—cabbage, broccoli, and kale were all the same species of plant, which I actually thought was pretty interesting—but it took almost a week for me to remember to look it up, and by that time we were already back home.

And that was when we were here for five days, not even a week. I'd never had to deal with *six weeks* of this ridiculousness.

I messaged Mom, who said to tell her parents she loved them. Since I had just seen her a few hours ago, there wasn't much else for me to say yet. I messaged Vicky to tell her that I had arrived, but she didn't answer, so I didn't really have much to do on my tablet. If it hadn't been about to be taken away from me, I probably would have left it alone in favor of a book. Instead, I ended up playing a game where I solved math puzzles to gobble up ghosts and turn into a mega-ghost. The game was for little kids, so the math problems were easy, but it was soothing, and I still had to aim to eat the ghosts, so there was *some* skill involved.

It wasn't long before Frank was heading off to the car with a tub of meatballs and sauce to bring home to Mom. Nana and Papa stood on the porch to wave goodbye.

"Bring my daughter with you when you come back!" called Papa.

"And stay longer!" added Nana.

"That's the plan!" Frank gave a cheesy thumbs-up out of the driver's side window and drove off.

"Okay," said Nana with her hand out, "time to hand over the screens."

"What?" exclaimed Becca, which was silly because we both already knew it was going to happen.

"We're not monsters," said Nana. "You'll have your tablets until lunch and after dinner. But in the afternoon, you'll be entertaining yourselves outdoors, and your electronics will be staying indoors. It's summer, it's beautiful out, and you're not stuck in your apartment building in the city. Enjoy it!"

"Can I read on the porch?" I asked.

"Of course," said Papa. "No one wants to keep you from reading."

"But maybe think about moving your body at some point," Nana added.

"Before you head outside, put your things in your room," said Papa. "We don't need to be stepping over them in the front hall."

I had almost forgotten one of the worst parts of staying at Nana and Papa's: The house only had two bedrooms, so when we stayed over, we had to share a room. Worse, the room only had a bunk bed.

"I call top bunk!" yelled Becca, running to the bedroom without her bag.

"I get the top bunk! I'm older!" I ran after her, lugging my bag with me.

She was already sitting on the top bunk when I got to the bedroom. The bottom bunk was wider, but there was no way I wanted to sleep with Becca over me.

"You always get the top bunk!" she said. "It's my turn!"

"I get the top bunk because I can climb the ladder in the dark."

"So can I!" said Becca. "You want to race?" Becca turned off the light.

"No racing in the bedroom." Papa flipped the light switch back on. "Especially not in the dark. Becca usually sleeps in the larger bottom bunk because she shares the bed with your mom, and she's smaller. But since it's just the two of you this time, why don't you switch it up?"

"But I'm *older*!" I said.

"All the more reason for you to be more mature and let your sister have the top bunk."

Becca's beaming smile was unbearable. At least Papa

made her go back to the front hall to get her bag.

Then we both got sent outside, Becca with her soccer ball and me with a book, for the beginning of a long summer of forced appreciation of the beautiful outdoors.

CHAPTER 4

In my lower-bunk bed the next morning, my brain started to whir up for the day. I had to remind myself half a dozen times that I wasn't at home. Mom wasn't there to give me a morning snuggle, but it also meant that I didn't need to get her a protein shake and make sure her water bottle was full. Once I left the bedroom, it was clear I was at Nana and Papa's. The house smelled like waffles, and I could hear Papa singing. Breakfast was his specialty.

"Don't even try getting cereal," said Becca, lying upside down on the living room couch, her legs sticking straight up and her head falling off the front. "Nana said that Papa's breakfast is *worth waiting for*. And it better be, 'cause my stomach's growling." At home, Becca and I usually ate cereal first thing in the morning, and I was already hungry too.

Becca was staring at her tablet, which she held in front of her, watching videos about kids building obstacle courses for one another. The big TV mounted to the wall was off. I didn't know why it was okay for us to use our tablets in the morning but not the TV, but I wasn't complaining. The afternoon was going to be worse.

I messaged Mom good morning and sent her a photo of a pretty sunrise. She sent me back a sun emoji, and then a cloud with a question mark. I found a photo of a sky where the clouds were white and fluffy in one corner but dark and stormy in the other. We did this sometimes where she would send me an emoji and I would send her back a picture to match.

"Ding-a-ling-a-ling!" Papa announced through the house as he mimed ringing a triangle. "Waffles waffles waffles! Get them 'fore they're cold and awfuls!"

"Finally!" Becca tossed her tablet onto the couch and jumped up.

"Rude!" I said, even though I was sort of feeling the same way. I sent Mom a photo of a tropical beach in response to the palm tree emoji she had sent, and told her I had to go for breakfast.

Nana was already seated at the dining room table as Papa brought in a giant pile of waffles and laid it in the center, surrounded by butter, whipped cream, real maple syrup, blueberries, and sliced strawberries.

"Don't worry, peaches will be in season soon enough," Papa said to me. He knew that peaches were my favorite fruit—possibly my favorite food—if you didn't count dessert.

"The berries look delicious," said Nana. She turned to Becca and me. "I *love* summer weekends. During the school year, Mr. Rossi over here is often drowning in papers to grade, especially by the end of the semester."

"And on summer weekdays," Papa continued the thought, "Mrs. Rossi needs to leave at seven thirty a.m. so she can be at the bank for her shift. And while I can be awake at that time, I am most certainly not a chef until at least eight."

"But summer weekends?" said Nana, gesturing at the food on the table as if it answered her question. "It looks amazing, and I'm ready to dig in."

Papa served each of us a fluffy waffle, leaving plenty

for seconds. Becca put a blueberry into each of the waffle dents. I preferred strawberries. Nana passed me the plastic jug of maple syrup with its tiny round handle and picture of a giant orange maple leaf, and I carefully poured some for myself and for Becca. If you let Becca pour her own, she'd end up with a waffle raft in a maple syrup sea. A squirt of whipped cream and breakfast was ready. I took a bite, then another, and for a few minutes, it wasn't so terrible that we were spending most of the summer in Massachusetts.

And after Sunday breakfast, it was time for the paper. Nana and Papa still got the daily newspaper delivered to their door, and on Sundays it was super thick and heavy. I always grabbed the comics first. They weren't all funny, but some of them were. Then I read the Marilyn vos Savant column in *Parade* magazine. She had the world's highest recorded IQ at 228, and I liked to read the questions and then come up with my own answers before I read hers. When we agreed, I felt really smart. After that, I was done with the paper. I left the table, Papa deep in the arts section and Nana working on the crossword.

I knew Vicky was visiting her aunt that morning, so I couldn't message her after breakfast. Or at least, she wouldn't message back. I wondered if she was getting in any reading time. I went up ten levels in *BakeItLast*, the game on my tablet where you make cakes and pies and sell them to forest creatures. Plus, I read half of a book, partly because I wanted to and partly because I wanted to have something to say if Nana or Papa said I was wasting my morning.

If the summer had been just the mornings, it would have been a breeze. But we all know that the afternoon follows the morning. After lunch, I was sitting with my tablet in the living room, waiting for the inevitable. I might have even served an acorn soufflé to a squirrel and made it to level 142 if Becca hadn't come into the living room screaming, "Chris, did you take my tablet?"

Before I could say that I had done no such thing, Nana came in from the kitchen to do it for me. "I put it away. You've already played with it enough for one morning. It's time to get some fresh air. Kids shouldn't be inside all summer." Nana clucked her tongue. "When I was young, we didn't have air-conditioning, and we certainly didn't have tablets and video streaming and gameboywhoozits and technowhatzits. You're a kid. You're supposed to be a *source* of energy, not a consumer."

"I'll go get my soccer ball," said Becca brightly, as if Nana wasn't being ridiculous. If Becca was disappointed, it wasn't in her voice. And given her inability to hide her feelings, it seemed she really was fine.

I tried not to let my irritation show when Nana said, "You too, Chris," but I must have let a little sigh escape when I handed over my tablet, because she gave me a *hmpph* and a lecture.

"When your mom was little, she was out all day long, from breakfast until dinner. Some days she'd stop in to grab a sandwich and a drink, usually with four or five other kids in tow, and then they'd be gone twenty minutes later. But it all worked out. Feeding half a dozen kids once a week wasn't much different from feeding one kid every day. I felt bad for Sarah Graper, though. She and her husband put in a pool one summer, and after that, her place was overrun with wet feet leaving puddles on the floor and pruned hands grabbing for ice pops."

I smiled quietly through Nana's reprimand-turned-trip-down-memory-lane. That was the best way to handle this sort of thing. As long as I wasn't being asked a direct question, I didn't need to say anything, and trying to get Nana to hurry up before she was done with her story just meant hearing a different story about why you shouldn't do that.

"All of which is to say"—Nana's signal that she was done reminiscing and back to chastising—"you should be out enjoying the air and the sunshine, relishing your youth."

"Yay, youth," I deadpanned.

"Go outside." Nana's voice was firm.

"Can I bring a book?"

"Bring a grand piano for all I care, as long as you play it outside."

I grabbed *Unidentified Suburban Object* and *Everlasting Nora* from the room I was sharing with Becca and went out into the summer heat. I didn't want to risk getting in trouble for needing to come inside in the middle of the afternoon for a new book.

I read on the porch while Becca ran around in the yard, interrupting me with cheers from a pretend audience whenever she did something she was especially proud of, which was way too often as far as I was concerned. She would run around in a circle with her hand out, as if she were high-fiving her adoring fans. She even tried to get me to high-five her the first few times until I threatened to throw my book at her and she threatened to tell Nana and Papa and I said that I wasn't really going to throw my book because I wanted to read it, not waste it on her.

I got a little break from Becca when she followed Papa into the vegetable garden. I had finished my book and was still in the glow of appreciating a fabulous story when she was back, telling me about how Papa planted beans where he had planted squash last year because of the different nutrients they needed from the dirt. Or, as she put it, the different *nutrimints* they needed. I didn't correct her.

I tried starting the new book, but I could tell right away that something bad was going to happen to the mom. I did read it later that summer, and it turned out to be an amazing story, but I was too worried about my actual mom that day to read about scary things happening to a mom in a book.

After dinner, I asked for my tablet back.

"You were on it all morning," said Nana, in a way that sounded like that meant I shouldn't want it now.

"You said we could have our tablets after dinner. Besides, I want to call Mom. She's having surgery in the morning, remember?"

"I wanna call Mommy too!" said Becca.

"That's not a bad idea," said Papa. "I'd love to talk to her too."

Soon we were gathered on the couch, trying to fit all four of our faces on the screen at once, waving at Mom in her bed back in New York and trading "I miss you"s and "I love you"s.

Mom remembered to ask me about GS72BC, and I was

proud to say I was two books ahead of schedule. She also listened to Becca talk about the soccer running moves she'd been practicing and even watched her demonstrate how she could balance the ball on her knee, which was the only thing Nana and Papa would let her do in the house. Nana and Papa took a turn with the tablet, wishing Mom the best for a quick and simple operation.

"I'll breathe more easily once you're on the other side of this," said Nana.

"No pressure," Mom joked.

"You know what I mean," said Nana.

"We're looking forward to you having your life back," said Papa.

Mom sighed. "I mean, recovery's gonna be a *@$#." Mom said that dealing with chronic pain deserved to be cursed about. "I'm still gonna have bad days. This isn't my first surgery, and it probably won't be my last."

We all sat in the silence of the word *surgery*, wondering who would break it. No surprise that it was Mom. "But you're right, I do usually feel better after recovery, and the doctor said the results for this one are promising."

The conversation got lighter after that, and soon Mom had us laughing about how Frank had messed up this morning and said *shocks and soes* instead of *socks and shoes*.

"It wasn't *that* funny," Frank harrumphed, but with a sparkle in her eye that said the grump only went an inch deep.

After we got off the call with Mom, I tried to call Vicky, but she didn't answer. So I sent her a picture of my reading log for the day and told her to call me back when she could talk.

Before I could finish a single order in *BakeItLast*, Nana asked whether we wanted to watch a movie.

"Movie! Movie! Movie!" Becca jumped around the room.

"Really?" I asked Nana. "I thought you hated screen time."

"I hate when all you kids do all day is stare at a screen and forget how to make your own entertainment," said Nana. "But family movie night? I've been doing that since I was a kid and we had to watch whatever movie was on TV that night."

"What if there wasn't anything good on?" asked Becca.

"Then we'd have to wait for another day."

"What did you watch then?"

"We watched each other chew our food." Nana made a ridiculous chewing face. Becca laughed and returned the look.

"Movie night?" Papa asked as he walked into the room, as if Nana and Becca weren't acting like two cows munching grass.

"Movie! Movie! Movie!" Becca jumped around again.

"Okay then, I'll make some popcorn. You choose the flick." Papa went to the kitchen and tossed a packet of popcorn into the microwave.

"So, what do you two want to watch?" asked Nana, scrolling through the kids' section on the TV.

"Penguin for the Win!" Becca screamed as the image of a penguin with a soccer ball popped onto the screen.

"Chris?"

"Sure." This was probably the 1,503,784th time Becca had watched *Penguin for the Win*, which was 1,503,783 more times than the movie deserved. But I didn't really care. I figured once Vicky was done with dinner or whatever, she'd message me and I'd go off and chat with her.

But then Nana took away my tablet because she said that one screen at a time was enough, and that if I wasn't interested in the movie, it was still light out and I could go take a walk if I wanted. So I watched the stupid movie about soccer-playing penguins and their walrus coach. At least the popcorn was good.

In bed that night, running my tongue over my freshly brushed teeth, checking for husks, I thought about Mom and whether she was as scared about the surgery as I was. Maybe more. If she could deal with that, I could deal with a summer of porch books and weird rules about screens.

CHAPTER 5

When Nana handed Becca and me our tablets the next morning, Frank had already sent a message saying that Mom was at the hospital getting prepped for surgery. By the time we read it, Mom was probably in the operating room, where she would be for at least four hours. Frank promised to update us as soon as there was any news. The morning went terribly slowly. Papa didn't make anything fancy for breakfast and Nana didn't go to her weekday morning job at the local bank. Instead, she deep cleaned the kitchen while Papa sat on the porch. He didn't even wander through the garden.

I couldn't concentrate to read, I wasn't interested in any of the games on my tablet, and Vicky still hadn't messaged me back.

Becca started watching annoying videos of people screaming as they threw water balloons at one another. I retreated to our room and started playing the next chapter in my audiobook, trying to drown out my thoughts about Mom and Vicky and Becca. But I couldn't even concentrate enough for Vidalia, so I put on some music and let the feelings wash over me in wave after wave of sadness and fear and anger and frustration.

At some point I fell asleep, and then Nana was knocking on the door to tell me that lunch was ready and it was time to get back out of bed. It was another long three hours before we heard from Frank, but Nana didn't make us go outside. At least, not until we heard about Mom.

"The surgery went textbook perfect," Frank said, once she called. "She's still asleep now, and she'll be groggy for a while, but I'm sure she's going to want to call you when she can. We'll talk again soon!"

At that, Nana sent us outside.

"But it's so hot," Becca said. She wasn't wrong. For once.

Nana clucked her tongue. "It's barely eighty degrees. If it breaks ninety, you can come in and I'll make lemonade."

Most of the time, Massachusetts wasn't really that hot and when we (mostly Becca, because she was the one running around all the time) complained that it was, we usually got a lecture about how it was good for the body to *bear a little challenge now and then, especially when you're young.* But ninety degrees was special, at least to Nana and Papa, who treated it as some sort of magical temperature. On the porch, a thermometer decorated with squirrels, a deer, and other not-to-scale woodland creatures decreed whether we'd suffer. Ninety degrees? *Okay, you can stay inside.* But 89.5? *Go out! A little sweat never hurt anyone!* So basically we were cooler when it was ninety degrees out than when it was eighty, because if it was ninety, we were in air-conditioning.

I sat on the porch and read while Becca played with her soccer ball. I was glad that Mom's surgery had gone well, but I still had trouble concentrating. The echoes of fear were still slipping through my brain, slithering through my thoughts. I hoped I would feel better after I saw her.

And I was. A little bit, anyway. Frank called Nana again once Mom was awake. She tried calling my tablet first, but I was in outside jail, where electronics were forbidden. At least Nana was reasonable enough to let us come in for the call.

"My babies!" Mom gushed. She was wearing a light blue robe and a goofy smile. I'd seen that look before, usually when her pain was extra bad and she'd taken her heavy-duty medication.

"Mommy!" Becca yelled. "How are you?"

"I've been worse," she said dazedly. "I've been better, but I've been worse."

"I hope they're treating you alright," said Nana.

"Me too," said Mom, as if she hadn't really heard the question.

Frank turned the camera to herself. "She's only been out of anesthesia for a little bit, and they've got her well medicated."

"Better than being in pain," said Nana.

"Absolutely," said Frank.

"Uh-hunh," Mom agreed.

"So, Becca," asked Frank, "how's the soccer practice been going?"

"I'm doing great." Becca beamed.

"She really is," Papa agreed. "You might have a professional athlete on your hands someday."

"That'd be nice," said Mom dazily.

"And how's the reading going?" Frank asked me.

"On target to finish!" I said. Or at least I was. I didn't know how Vicky was doing.

"Good for you!" Mom mumbled.

"Chris was on the porch all afternoon yesterday, reading away," said Nana proudly, but then added, "Now if we could just get her head out of a book long enough to notice it's summer."

"Summer, summer, bo-bummer," sang Mom, her voice fading along with her consciousness. "Banana-fana-fo-fummer."

"I think that's our cue to get off the phone and let you get some rest," said Papa.

"Agreed," said Frank.

So we said good night to Mom, even though it was still the afternoon, and then Nana shooed us back outside like we would get sick with some sort of in-the-house-during-the-summer flu or something. Even though *she* stayed inside. Papa came out to work on his garden, though, and Becca went to join him, so at least I didn't have to listen to the sounds of Becca playing with her round sports thing. And now that I had seen Mom after surgery, even if she was a little silly, I was able to concentrate, and I finished my book, plus a graphic novel, before we got called in to eat.

When I got my tablet back after dinner, there was a message from Vicky hours ago saying *hi*. I messaged back, worried that she would be eating dinner, but she responded immediately.

>Chris: hi
>Vicky: oh wow. I'm just waking back up. I came home from YETT and crashed. I took like a 3 hour nap
>Chris: what's YETT?
>Vicky: Youth Empowerment Through Theater
>Chris: oh, your camp. how bad was it?
>Vicky: actually, it was kind of fun.

Chris: oh

Vicky: I mean, not, like, talking books with you fun, but better than sitting home alone

Chris: oh, ok

Vicky: wanna video?

Chris: yes!!

When we connected, Vicky told me about a game they had played at camp. They had gotten in a circle and one of the counselors mimed an imaginary ball in their hands. They threw it to another counselor, and the ball was suddenly heavy. She threw it to the third counselor, who acted like it was sticky and had gotten caught in her hair. Then they started passing it around the room to the campers. When Vicky got it, she pretended it was a ball of light so bright that she couldn't look at it without blinding herself.

"But this one kid, Kira, did the best," Vicky said, as I watched the minutes tick by in the corner of the screen. "When she got the ball, she pretended it splattered all kinds of goo all over her and kept picking the goo off long after it was her turn. And when it was time to play this mirror game, I got paired up with Kira and our moves were way funnier than anyone else's. Like, we were disco dancing while some of the other teams were still trying to coordinate moving their hands up and down at the same time."

"Sounds like you had a good time," I said.

"Sorry to ramble on. It's just there's a lot going on here."

There was a lot going on here too. Or at least a lot going on back home with Mom that I wanted to tell Vicky.

But before I could tell her any of it, she cried out, "Oh no! My mom's calling me. We're going out for dinner, so I gotta go. But maybe I can message in the car."

And then she was gone. I hadn't told her about Mom. I hadn't gotten to update her on the ways Becca was being the worst. We hadn't even told each other what we were reading. I messaged her that Mom was okay after surgery, and she sent back a bunch of happy emojis, but when I told her about the two books I'd read today, she didn't tell me what she'd read.

It's not that I needed Vicky. I was fine on my own. But something didn't feel right.

CHAPTER 6

Bounce bounce bounce bounce bounce.

Becca was kicking her soccer ball against the side of the back porch, over and over and over again. I was finishing up the *Rogue Space* book I had started yesterday so I could get on to my new book for the day. Or at least, I was trying to, but the thud of the ball had me reading the same line over and over.

"Do you really have to do that here?" I complained.

Becca stopped for a second. "Not if you would play with me."

"I promise you this," I responded. "I will *never* play soccer with you."

"I know."

"Then why do you ask?"

"Because I want to do *something* with you. You may not like me, but I like you."

Ouch. Not that it wasn't true, but it didn't feel great to know that she knew it.

Becca resumed her *bounce, bounce, bounce.*

I hate soccer. I completely loathe everything to do with it. I always kick too early or too late. Plus, I'm a slow runner so someone else always gets to the ball first anyway. I knew kicking the ball back and forth with Becca didn't involve running, so that part wouldn't matter. Except that Becca could already run and kick at the same time while I tripped over my own feet whenever they made us try that kind of thing in gym class. So, no, I didn't want to kick the ball back and forth with her. Or have her kick the ball at me and then chase it when I missed it, looking like a fool next to my baby sister to anyone watching.

Not that anyone was watching. Occasionally we'd see an adult or two walking down the road, sometimes with a dog. But I had never seen another kid around. I dreamed of another kid showing up who liked soccer, and who would have invited her to play in *their* backyard.

Bounce bounce bounce.

I returned to *Rogue Space* and read the same sentence over and over. I was just about ready to throw the book right at Becca's feet when Papa emerged from the back door.

"Good form, Becca!" he called.

"Thanks. I'm aiming for the same spot each time."

"You've got a good rhythm going. I can hear it inside."

"Sorry, Papa." She put out her foot to catch the soccer ball and it scooted to a stop without a hint of her losing her balance. *Yes, this is it*, I thought. *Papa is finally going to make her stop.*

"No sweetie, you keep at it. I just wanted to come out here and compliment you." Papa turned to me. "And how are you doing, Chris? Enjoying your book?"

"Trying to, but I can't concentrate with Becca's thudding. Can I come inside?"

"Slim chance." He smiled at my nerve, but with a firmness that said not to keep trying. "Why don't you go for a walk? The trail behind the house is nice and shady, and the creek is lovely this time of year." He pointed to a break in the trees beyond the grass yard.

I must have made a face because Papa added, "Plus, you'll get some privacy. Becca's not old enough to head down there alone, but I trust you, and I think you could use some time to yourself."

"Fine," I said. I wasn't sure it was fine, but I was pretty sure I didn't have a choice.

Whenever we visited, Papa tried to get me to walk down to the stream behind the house with him, but Mom had always been here to say it was fine to read a book on the porch instead, and would distract Becca with bubbles or something. Now, it looked like my options were the path or to read the same sentence with every skull-penetrating *bounce*.

Papa shooed me with his hands, and whispered, "And get out of here before your sister sees you leaving."

He made a good point. If Becca knew I was going on a walk, she would want to go with me. I was actually surprised he wasn't going to make me wait for her.

Papa went over to bounce the ball a few times with Becca. I dashed off before she noticed.

I kicked small rocks as I walked down the narrow path, watching them skip left and right. I could still hear the *bounce bounce bounce* behind me. It faded as I made my way between the trees, and it wasn't more than a hundred feet before I ran into a wider dirt path running to the left and right, and a stream directly ahead of me, flowing to the right. The *bounce bounce bounce* was gone, in favor of the sound of water dancing over itself.

I made my way through a patch of sticks and leaves up to the edge of the stream. I listened as the water spilled over the pebbled bed with a *burble, lurble, plurble, blurp*. I'd heard of a babbling brook before, but I'd never actually heard one speak in real life. Or maybe it was a chattering creek. Either way, the water was only a few inches deep here, and it made me think of how we learned in science that the shallower the water, the faster the flow.

I picked my way back to the path and followed it upstream. The water was quieter there, and when I approached the stream bank again, the water looked darker and way deeper. Maybe a foot. Maybe two. And a bit farther ahead, a fallen tree draped across the stream like an image out of a novel about a kid with a secret reading spot in the woods.

I wanted to be that kid. And in wanting to, I was that

kid. I made my way to the tree bridge, my socks and shoelaces picking up tiny fuzzy plant balls with each step. There was probably a name locals called those little fuzzies—*sock stickers* or something—and I would know it if I were that kid in a book. The water was shallower again here, and the creek chattered with a *trickle brickle pilk*.

The fallen tree jutted out at a ninety-degree angle about two feet off the ground, in two main branches: a larger lower one to walk on and, above that, a narrower one to hold onto for balance. Right in the middle of the stream, the lower branch split in two, forming what looked like a cozy seat, just waiting to be enjoyed.

I transferred my book to my left hand and tested the tree, first with my hand, and then with my foot. It seemed stable. A couple of small ants, but only individuals—no lines to find marching across my skin.

I grabbed on to a stub of a low branch and hoisted myself up. Once I was on the tree, it was a few easy steps out to where the water was *burble-plurp*ing underneath me. I settled into place, and it was perfect. My feet were hanging a couple of inches from the water, and there was even a broken bit of branch to use as a crook for my book. It was so beautiful that I kind of wished I had gone on a walk with Papa one of the times he had asked before. Kind of. But walking along the stream would get boring. Reading by the water was much better.

I settled into place and finished my novel. The ending was disappointing, but it still counted for GS72BC. It turned out that the big mysterious sad thing in the main character's life was that her sister had died. If there's one thing that I don't want to read about in a book, it's a dead sibling. Not because anyone close to me has died, but because I had a hard time sympathizing with all these kids who loved their siblings more than anyone else in the world. It happened all the time in books, and I wanted to ask all these authors why they were so obsessed with kids dying.

And the sibling was almost always a twin or older. No one was mourning their eight-year-old little sister's death in these books. Which made sense to me. Eight-year-old younger sisters were unbearable alive . . . but I also knew I'd be in big trouble if anyone ever heard me say something like that out loud.

Once I was done with my book, I watched the water ripple below my feet. It was actually pretty soothing, and I watched it for a while, the shadows of my legs swinging and the sparkles where the sun reached down between the leaves.

I had a feeling I would be coming back here a lot this summer.

CHAPTER 7

The first week didn't go by quickly, but it wasn't too miserable. Breakfast, hang out and read inside, lunch, get kicked out of the house, read by the creek, go back to the house for a snack, more creek-side reading, dinner, tablet time, TV or a movie with Nana and Papa, and then bed. Wake up and do it again.

We did get to talk to Mom every night. Becca liked to call at her bedtime, and it was nice to talk with her. She wasn't as out of it after that first night, but she was tired a lot, so most of our calls were quick.

I usually got to video call, or at least message, with Vicky too, but our conversations were almost as short. When she wasn't busy with YETT, she was busy with family. Over the weekend, Vicky's cousin had been in from out of town, and even when her family wasn't showing her around New York, they were hanging out together. It sounded like she was having fun, but we had barely talked about GS72BC since I had gotten here. I was five books ahead of target already, but I had no idea how many books she had read. She did ask about Mom, which was nice, even if there wasn't much to say except that she was still in bed and healing.

I also got to check out the Leverett Library with Papa and Becca. It wasn't the St. George branch of the New York Public Library at home, where the entire basement was for kids and kids' books, but for a one-story building, I was impressed. The main room was shaped in an L, and kids' books took up one half of the L. Middle grade filled an entire wall, including four bookcases just for graphic novels. And across from them, there were just as many picture books. There were lots of recent titles too, not dusty rows of some old librarian's even older favorites from when they were a kid. They had the classics, of course, like *Charlotte's Web*, but there were also lots of new books. I'd read lots of them, but there were bunches more I'd never heard of.

Not even Becca complaining that the library was boring could bother me as I prepared my stack to take home with us. According to the library's website, a patron can borrow up to fifty books, but Papa said I had to keep it to twenty, and that either he or Nana would drive me back as often as I needed. Soon Papa was helping me stuff a treasure of stories that would last me through the next weeks into a pair of canvas bags.

Having twenty books to read myself wasn't the same as having twenty books to talk about with Vicky, but it was still twenty books.

A week to the day after we had arrived, Nana dished out a heaping scoop of mashed potatoes for each of us at dinner. Roasted chicken and a pile of green beans were already on each of our plates. She served everyone, even Papa.

"Grew the beans myself." Papa nodded with pride, took one in his fingertips, and popped it into his mouth. "And dressed perfectly, Cindy."

The green beans were tangy, crunchy, and cold. Not steamed and buttered the way Mom made them. They were really good, and the fact that Becca wouldn't touch them sealed the deal for me—I ate every last one. The chicken and potatoes were delicious too. If Nana was old-fashioned about things like kids playing outside, at least she was also old-fashioned about being an amazing cook.

"Either of you is welcome to help me out in the garden anytime you want," said Papa. "I'm planning to get out there in the morning."

"I want to!" said Becca.

"And what about you, Chris?"

"Nah, that's okay." If Becca was helping, I was out. Besides, I'd helped Mom plant a garden once a few years ago, and from what I remembered, it involved a lot of moving dirt around . . . and it turned out that dirt was *heavy*. Maybe that was good exercise for a future soccer pro, but especially in the summer heat, it sounded like a cruel punishment. The disappointed look on Papa's face, though, made me glad that I was able to follow up with, "I want to get back to the creek."

Papa's face softened. "Well, in that case, do your thing. I'm sure one extra set of hands in the garden will be enough to deal with."

"Sounds like you had a good day," Nana said to me in a way that pointed out that all the days here in Massachusetts were good and I had just noticed.

"It was alright," I said. I didn't want them to think I liked being outside all day long. But if I was going to be outside, reading alongside a burbling creek seemed like the way to go.

"And you got some good soccer practice in," Papa said to Becca.

"Yeah, but I had to do all the drills myself." Becca poked at the green beans on her plate before picking up another forkful of potatoes. "It's so boring being just me all day."

"Well, you'll be in the garden tomorrow," said Nana. "That'll be fun, right?"

"Yeah, but that's different."

"Hey now! What am I, chopped liver?" Papa's face started out stern, but quickly broke into a grin that let on that he was only pretending to be offended.

"I just mean you're not a kid!"

"You could always play with Chris," Nana offered, like I was a serving of potatoes.

"No!" Becca and I said at the same time.

"I wish there were kids around," said Becca.

"I do too," said Nana. "It's important to play with other kids. But we bear the burdens we are given."

"Hunh?" asked Becca.

"She means *deal with it*," I said.

"I most certainly do not." Nana gave me a dirty look. "But I do mean that sometimes we need to figure out ways to have fun in less-than-ideal situations. Look at Chris. She manages to have a good time on her own."

"That's not fair! Chris is . . ." Becca stopped.

The conversation stopped.

For a moment, it felt like the whole world had stopped.

"I'm what?"

"You know. You just . . . you don't make friends real fast."

"Your sister is independent, and that's something to admire," said Nana.

Nana said it nicely, but it was true that I didn't have a lot of friends, and that I usually didn't know what to do when I met someone new. It was true, but that didn't give Becca the right to say it.

As if that wasn't enough, that night I had the worst call with Vicky yet.

"Have you finished the Vidalia trilogy?"

"No."

I gasped out loud. "What happened?"

"Honestly? I read the first one, and it was okay, but not, like, so good that it made me want to read another two books. I like real-world stuff more than fantasy. I mean," Vicky stumbled over her words, "not that real-world stuff is better. It's just what I like, you know?"

"I guess." I couldn't really imagine not liking Vidalia, but there were plenty of books I didn't like, even ones Vicky had given to me.

"Also?" Vicky hesitated, as if she was about to say another thing I wouldn't want to hear. "They're really long. *Swords & Secrets* took me all week to finish."

"But you're a fast reader!"

"Yeah, when I love what I'm reading. Plus, I had stuff to do with my family, and now there's YETT. Even if I was reading regular-sized books, I don't know how I'd keep up. What if— Now hear me out, okay?" Vicky braced herself for my disagreement before I even knew what I was disagreeing with, which only made me more disagreeable. "What if we made some changes to GS72BC?"

"What's wrong with GS72BC?"

"Nothing . . . exactly."

"Well, if it's nothing, then why are you bringing it up?"

"I just wonder whether the number has to be seventy-two."

"Of course it has to be seventy-two. That's how many days we have off for summer! You can always read picture books to catch up."

"I don't want to read a bunch of picture books," said Vicky.

"Some of them are good! Remember the one about the upside-down turtle?" Our librarian had read us a story at the beginning of the year about how helping can just mean being there with someone when they can't turn themselves over, instead of suggesting how you would turn yourself over if you were a turtle.

"Yeah, some of them are," said Vicky. "But I don't want to have to read a bunch of them just because I said I would read a ridiculous number of books."

I didn't think seventy-two was a ridiculous number. Big, yes, but not ridiculous. If it weren't a challenge, it wouldn't be the Great Summer 72 Book Challenge. It would just be the Regular Hot Season Whatever-Number-You-Feel-Like-It Book Not-Challenge, and while anything involving books is good, *Regular* was not *Great*.

I asked Vicky, "Are you saying you don't want to do GS72BC?"

"I was thinking more like GS24BC?" Vicky's face looked like she couldn't decide whether to smile or not. Mine knew not to. "I love reading! You know I do! It's just . . ."

Vicky paused. I knew I probably should have waited for her to continue, but I was annoyed.

"It's just what?" I could hear the accusation in my own voice, that her reason had better be good.

"It's just that I have other things to do this summer! Like YETT!"

That did not count as good. "I thought it was only two afternoons a week," I said.

"Well, yeah, the classes are, but we usually go to the diner afterward. And we're gonna start getting together on Mondays and Wednesdays to practice our lines."

"Who's 'we'?"

"Shayla, Jay, Niko, and me. The kids in my practice group."

"So you'd rather spend time with strangers that your mom's making you hang out with than read?"

"They're not strangers. They're my friends."

Vicky was supposed to be like me. We didn't make friends easily. That was part of our thing. And now she'd gone and made not one, not two, but *three* new friends.

Plus, maybe other friends who weren't in her practice group.

"*I'm* your friend," I reminded her.

"You're also not here. I'm not like you, Chris. I can't just spend my whole summer lonely by myself in my room. I need to see people."

"I see people," I said softly. But Chris was right. I could go days at a time without talking to anyone if Mom would let me.

"Do you not want me to have other friends?" Vicky asked. I couldn't tell whether she sounded surprised, angry, or hurt. Maybe all three.

"No," I told her. "I mean yes. I mean, I want you to have other friends."

"I still wanna read and talk books this summer. I just thought we could do things a little differently."

"I'll think about it."

And I did think about it. All night long. I thought about just how much I hated it. I didn't want things to change. Things had changed enough already with me being here and her doing YETT. We had come up with the idea for GS72BC together, and we had been so excited about it.

I wanted Vicky to have other friends. I really did, if that's what she wanted. But I didn't want her other friendships to affect ours. I didn't want to lose my best friend.

PART II

CHAPTER 8

The first time I saw Mia Yaring, I was sitting on my perch over the water. I was deep in a book, and the only reason I looked up was because I heard rustling footsteps. She had already passed, and I didn't think she'd seen me.

CHAPTER 9

The next day, I heard her coming and I waved from my tree perch. She waved back. Then we both looked away from each other, or at least I know I did, and by the time I looked back, she was gone.

CHAPTER 10

The day after that, I had barely gotten three pages into my book when I heard someone say "hi."

I looked up, and there she was.

"Hi," I said back.

We stared at each other for a moment. Then another.

"My name's Mia."

She looked like she was about my age, and she had dark brown hair back in a loose braid, with some wispy bits around her face.

"I'm Chris." I looked down at the space next to me on my tree perch and gestured. "Want to sit?"

"Nah," said Mia. "I gotta get back to my grandma's."

"Oh, okay."

She shrugged, then I shrugged, and she walked off like it wasn't a big deal, but it was like feeling a bit of myself walk off and I knew I needed to get it back.

CHAPTER 11

The fourth day, I was prepared with a foolproof plan. I had a hard time concentrating on my book. Mia had passed by about the same time every day that week. That didn't mean she would again, but she did, and I was ready.

"On your way to your grandma's?" I asked.

"Yeah."

"Mind if I walk with you?"

"Sure."

It wasn't an extremely complicated plan.

"So," I asked, "why are you out at the same time every day?"

"My grandma is making me deliver lunch to this old guy, and then I have to come back to help with chores." So she passed by twice a day.

"Oh. You live with her?"

"Nah. I'm just here for the summer. I live with my mom, but she's traveling for work."

"Me too!" I say. "The just-here-for-the-summer part, anyway. My pain-in-the-butt little sister is here too."

"Little siblings are the worst." Mia hopped over a tree branch, and I followed.

"You have a little sister too?"

"No, but I have a little brother."

"How old?"

"Seven."

"The worst age! I should know. My sister's eight."

I told Mia about the time that Becca had strung yarn all around our room like a spiderweb, with special attention paid to my bed. I had still been asleep, and when I woke up, I was trapped on my mattress. I had to call for my mom to rescue me with scissors.

"Sounds like eight's pretty bad too," said Mia.

"Oh, that was last year."

Mia told me about before she had left for the summer, when her brother used her books as building blocks and got them all out of order.

"That's not *so* bad." I mean, I wouldn't want someone touching my books either, but Becca had made a giant mess with the string, and I had really needed to pee when I woke up.

"Yeah, but I had just spent a month sorting them by genre and by whether I had read them or not, and making the best rainbow I could out of each section."

"Oh! That *is* way worse." If Becca had done something like that to me, I probably would have screamed and wanted to throw every single book at her face.

"He's staying at our house with our aunt, but they sent me away so she wouldn't have to deal with us fighting. I'm kind of glad to be here alone for the summer, if it means I don't have to see him," Mia confessed. "But don't tell my mom I said that! Officially, I am offended that they sent me away."

"Your secret is safe with me." I wish I could have been sent away without Becca.

Mia then asked me what I was reading, and I showed her the cover, which showed two kids riding a pterodactyl through a Brooklyn neighborhood.

"Is it any good?"

"It's amazing!"

"Can I borrow it when you're done?"

"Totally," I said.

"Thanks."

"What's your favorite book?"

"What's yours?" asked Mia.

"I asked you first!"

"On the count of three."

"1-2-3—*Sword & Secrets!*" I said, while she said, "1-2-3—*Roses & Thorns!*"

"Omigod!" we both said at the same time. *Swords & Secrets* was the first book in the Magical Mysterious Vidalia trilogy, and *Roses & Thorns* was the last. It was hard to find someone else who had read the first one, much less all three. We gabbed about Vidalia until we reached her grandma's house.

And then it was me, walking home by myself, delighted with my new friend.

That evening, after dinner and our call with Mom, Becca asked me to check her for ticks. I hated ticks. I hated everything about ticks. I hated the very idea of ticks. Nana once used the word *burrowing* about ticks, and after that I couldn't even think about them without imagining one tunneling under my skin, leaving a raised strip along my body like a groundhog in a cartoon. Nana explained that it was just the tip of the head that might get in, and that it certainly couldn't tunnel, but the idea of any part of an insect on me, much less in me, made my skin crawl like it was covered in insects.

"Can't it wait until the end of the chapter?" I asked.

"No, you need to check now, before I get Lyme disease. Nana said you had to!"

Nana said we should check for the little jerks daily. We'd been checking for ticks for three weeks without finding anything. I didn't see why it was so important.

"You're not going to get Lyme disease in the next ten minutes. Besides, if there were a tick on you, you'd know it!"

"Not true. Nana said that it doesn't hurt when they bite, so we might not even notice it. And she said that the sooner you find the tick, the better."

"Okay, fine." I put down my book.

"And look closely. Nana said they were small, so if

you're not looking closely, you might miss them."

"I'm looking closely!"

"Look closely-er!"

"If I were looking any closer, *I'd* be biting you."

I checked all up and down Becca's back, and even made her lift her hair to make sure there was nothing on her neck.

"All clear."

"You want me to check you too?" Becca asked. "Nana said it was better to check each other than ourselves."

"Nah, I'm good."

It was one thing for me to check my kid sister's back. It was another for her to look at mine. I had already started to grow, and even though she would only be looking at my back, it made me feel exposed. Besides, I hadn't been playing who-knows-where all afternoon. I'd been mostly on the tree bridge reading, and I made sure to wear long pants and tucked them into my socks even though it was hot out, so ticks were unlikely.

I wondered if when Mia and her brother were both here, he made her check him for ticks too.

CHAPTER 12

The next day was Saturday. I wasn't sure whether Mia delivered lunch on the weekends, but I figured that people need to eat every day, and I was right, because Mia walked by, same time as usual. I put a marker in my book and climbed off my reading perch to join her on her walk. Our walk.

"So, why did your mom dump you here in the land of old people?" Mia asked casually, like it was a question that people asked all the time. Given that we had both been dumped here by our moms, I guessed it wasn't all that unusual. Most people started conversations with at least a hello first, but we felt so close it was like we were continuing our conversation from the day before.

I told her about Mom's neck, and the surgery, and how Mom was going to need to rest afterward.

"But she'll be better after that, right?" Mia asked.

I shrugged. "Probably. She was better after surgery last time. But then sometimes she gets worse again.

Like now, she really doesn't get out of bed except to use the bathroom, and even then, she's supposed to use a walker."

"How does she eat?"

"In bed. We bring her meals."

"So, like, breakfast, lunch, and dinner in bed, but terrible."

"Pretty much. Well, when she has an appetite anyway. Sometimes she just has protein drinks. What about you? Where's your mom for the summer? Didn't you say she traveled for work?"

"Wellllllllllll." The way she drew out the word almost made it seem like she was going to say that her mom was home recovering from surgery for chronic pain too, but it wasn't that at all. "Actually, my mom's a singer. Like, professionally."

Mia got more amazing by the moment. I couldn't think of a cooler job for a mom to have.

"And she has a gig for the summer, singing on a cruise ship."

It just got cooler. "Wait, what?"

"Yeah, she's sailing to the Caribbean ten times this summer."

"Why aren't you with her?" I tried not to share my exasperation, but I don't think I did a very good job.

"She's an entertainer on the ship, but she's still staff. She has a roommate and everything. And there's no way she could pay for a room for all of us. Cruises are expensive."

That made sense. I had watched a show about what it was like to work on a cruise ship, and it definitely wasn't as glamorous as vacationing on one.

"My brother and I went for a week once last year with my grandma, though."

"It must have been amazing."

"It was alright. I mean, watching the water was really cool, but mostly the cruise was meant for adults who want to drink and watch lounge singers, not for kids who are looking for a quiet space to escape and read a book away from their baby brother."

"So basically this place but on the water," I said.

"Something like that."

"It's still a pretty cool job. My mom's a baker when her body lets her."

"Now *that's* cool!" Mia said. "I'll bet she makes the most delicious treats."

"She does!"

We let a comfortable silence fall between us. One that wasn't hard to break either.

"I don't usually like talking about my mom with people, because they get all weird about it. When I tell them she can't work right now, they say *sorry* in low, serious voices, as though my mom were dead or something."

"Well, I'm not, like, happy that your mom can't work," Mia said.

"Of course not! Neither am I. But people are so uncomfortable with bad news that they turn it into tragic news."

"That sounds stressful."

I thought about that. "You're right! I'm already dealing with my own stuff about my mom, and then I suddenly have to calm people down from their own ableism. It's not fair. Not all the news about my mom is terrible either. She's having surgery. That means she's going to have more good days again soon."

Mia nodded, like she knew that point was important, but that it didn't solve everything.

"She's never going to be the average person's idea of *fine*. She's always going to have to think about how things affect her body more than most people do. She's going to have to say no to things and sometimes that sucks. But people get so caught up in their own worries that they don't even stop to ask me what I'm thinking about."

Mia blinked slowly three times. Then she asked, "What are you thinking about?"

"Well, I'm worried about my mom and I hate that she's in pain!"

"Of course. What else?" Mia asked, guiding me through my own thoughts.

"I hate that we miss out on fun times because Mom can't go out to a lot of places."

"And?"

"And I worry that her girlfriend Frank is going to get sick of taking care of her and us and will leave someday."

Mia kept nodding. "And?"

"And, you know what I miss? When Mom worked at the bakery, she brought something home most nights. Sometimes it was just bread to go with dinner, but usually it was something sweet—a couple of cookies all the way up to an entire chocolate cake the day that some customer didn't come in to pick up his special order. We even sang happy birthday to Nina, the name on the cake."

Mia gasped. "No more chocolate cake? Now that *is* a loss."

"I'm not saying it's the *worst* part of it," I said.

"But sometimes it is the little things that really do add up."

"Yeah." I sighed. "Like hugging Mom without worrying that I'm going to make her pain worse."

"Well, you can always hug me," Mia said, holding out her arms. I met her squeeze with my squeeze, like we could bring ourselves closer emotionally by holding each other tighter.

Mia let go, her smiling face reflecting mine. She laughed and then started skipping down the path. I laughed and skipped after her until we were both out of breath. By then, we were nearly back at my perch, where we said our daily goodbyes and Mia headed back to her grandmother's house.

I messaged Vicky after dinner to ask whether she wanted to video call, but she didn't answer for an hour, and even then she said it would be better just to message.

>Me: what's wrong
>
>Vicky: nothing
>
>Me: are you stuck with family again

It was a couple of minutes before she responded. Maybe one of her aunts had asked her a question about what colleges she was thinking about, even though we weren't even in middle school yet.

Vicky: no

Me: then where are you

Vicky: Jay's house

Me: who's Jay

Vicky: from my YETT group. they're super cool and they have a pool

Vicky: Shayla and Niko are here too

Me: isn't it late

Vicky: we're having a sleepover!

Vicky: we're having so much fun!

Vicky: sorry I don't mean to brag

Me: it's ok

Me: I made a new friend too

Vicky: Really? I'm so happy for you

Vicky: what's she like

Me: her name is Mia and she's really nice

Me: she has an annoying little brother and she loves to read

Me: and she's staying here with her grandmother

Vicky: wow, she's like a perfect match for you

Me: don't worry, you're still my best friend

Vicky: awesome

Vicky: gotta go

And then she was gone. She didn't ask how Mom was doing. She didn't even say I was her best friend back.

CHAPTER 13

A few nights later, Nana portioned pulled pork with barbecue sauce, cornbread, and a heap of dark, shiny greens onto a set of plates in the kitchen and then called us to each grab our own to eat at the table in the backyard. She called it a traditional Southern dinner, and the pork was delicious, but the greens were pretty funky looking.

"I don't like the dollar greens," I said, remembering what Nana had called them.

"They're *collard* greens," Becca announced proudly. "It starts with a *c*, and the *d*'s at the end. I read it on the sign in Papa's garden."

Papa nodded in affirmation. "Easy to farm, and they're so good for you!" He loaded a pile onto his fork and stuffed them into his mouth with a grin.

"Blecch," Becca declared with just as much confidence.

"How would you know?" I asked. "You didn't even try them."

"You're not eating yours." Becca pointed at my plate.

"Yeah, because I know I don't like them. Because I tried them." I'd taken a bite, like I'd promised Mom I would do with all of Nana's cooking. Or at least, I'd touched a single bit to my tongue and my tongue had told me it was unpleasantly bitter, so I removed it.

"Well, you have two choices," said Nana. "You can skip the collard greens and then skip dessert, or you can eat now and then join us for ice cream when we're done."

"Mommy never makes us eat collard greens!" Becca stuck out her lower lip.

"Yeah, but she makes us eat spinach." I wasn't entirely sure why I was taking Nana's side in this, other than because it wasn't Becca's side. I mean, I didn't want to eat bitter goo leaves either.

"Collard greens are a great source of vitamins," Nana announced, as if that excused their taste.

Papa leaned over with his hand shielding his lips and spoke in a false whisper. "And if you mix them up with the pork and follow it up with a bit of buttered cornbread, you'll barely notice them."

Nana opened her mouth to protest, but thought better

of it when she saw Becca give it a try. A bit of greens topped with pork and then a bite of cornbread. Becca chewed a few times, then put out her thumb sideways. As she continued to chew, her thumb slowly turned upward. She swallowed and took another bite.

Under normal circumstances, Becca's appreciation would be enough to make me skeptical, but I had already seen the caramel ice cream in the freezer. So I gave it a chance, and Papa was right. The spicy sweetness of the barbecue sauce hid the texture and bitterness of the greens, and the crunchy-edged cornbread sang a little song in my mouth.

"So," said Papa, "how were your days?"

"I kicked the soccer ball a hundred and three times in a row!" said Becca. She had spent the day in the driveway, kicking the ball into the cement foundation of the house and kicking it again when it rebounded. *Thud. Thud. Thud.* All day long. I don't know how Nana and Papa didn't get a headache and yell at her to stop.

"Congratulations!" said Nana. "Sounds like a real accomplishment. What do you think, Chris?"

"I think I had to listen to Becca kick the soccer ball a hundred and three times in a row."

Nana gave me a look. "Do you want to say something different to your sister?" It was a demand, not a question.

"Congratulations," I muttered.

"I wouldn't have to do solo practice if there were other kids around to play with," Becca complained.

"Why don't you play with your sister?"

Becca and I both looked at Nana like she was some sort of alien who had never met either of us.

"What about your day, Chris?" said Papa.

"My day was okay, I guess. I hung out down by the creek. Reading, mostly." I thought about Mia, and how we had tried to guess each other's favorite Vidalia villains.

"Reading you're *supposed* to do by yourself!" Becca yelled. "You're not supposed to make friends to read. But me, I need friends!"

"Yeah, well, I wasn't by myself." I was sick of hearing about how Becca was the one who made friends, like I was some sort of lonely bog creature.

"What's that supposed to mean?" asked Becca.

"It means I made a friend. Her name is Mia. She loves to read, and her little brother is *almost* as annoying as you."

"Well, that's delightful news!" said Nana, managing to ignore the insults Becca and I had just launched at each other. She turned to Becca. "See, there are kids about. You just have to be patient. Chris made a friend. I'm sure you can too. Maybe you can even meet Mia's brother."

"Oh," I said, "he's not here this summer."

Becca glared at me from across the table, as if she was angry at me that I had made a friend and she hadn't. And as if it were my fault Mia's brother wasn't here. Why shouldn't I make a friend? I went exploring instead of kicking the soccer ball against a wall all day. She probably annoyed away any kids who might otherwise play with her with her incessant *pum-pum-pum*.

CHAPTER 14

I was sitting on my creek tree perch the next afternoon, more mind-wandering than reading, when I looked up from my book and saw Mia approaching.

"Hey!" we said at the same time.

"Come on out." I motioned Mia onto the log. Usually we walked on the path together, but there was plenty of room for a second kid body.

"I'd rather not" was all Mia said before taking a seat on a rock the size and approximate shape of a giant turtle. I hadn't noticed the big rock there before, but it certainly looked like a comfortable seat.

"Why not?"

"Look at your socks!"

I looked down at the sock sticker things that coated my socks and shoelaces. "Yeah, I keep getting them."

"See that patch there?" Mia pointed vaguely in the direction of a cluster of wide, flat leaves close to the ground between her and me. "Walk through that patch for ten seconds and you'll spend ten minutes picking them off."

She was right about the time it took to pull off every last little green ball. They wanted to travel with you. Great for seed spreading. Terrible for socks.

"By the way, what do you call them?" I asked.

"I don't know what their real name is. My grandma just calls them sock stickers."

"I knew it!"

"You knew what?"

"Just, I knew they'd have a cool local name." I didn't tell her that it was the exact name I had thought of. It sounded too much like I was making it up to impress her or something. Or that I was impressed with myself for figuring it out. Either way, I didn't like how it made me seem, so I left it out.

We talked about how hot it was, what we had eaten for breakfast, and what we were reading. I was reading *The Antiracist Kid*. Mia was reading the *Rogue Space* book I'd finished at the start of the trip. Somehow, she hadn't known that the *Rogue Space* universe included books.

"So I'm thinking that the Bzorki are going to find out that Ta'mara is half-Garantulan, but that Ta'mara is going to reveal that the emperor is her Bzorki mother," Mia theorized.

"Do you want me to tell you whether you're right or not? You told me not to spoil it for you."

Mia gave a resigned "no."

Then she told me about her grandmother, who insisted on calling her Maria. *"It's a beautiful name and you should learn to appreciate it,"* Mia mimicked.

"Ugh!" I gasped with dismay. "That sounds like my one aunt who calls me *Christie*." I paused for Mia to make a face, which she nailed. "And when I asked her not to call me that, she said *'At least I didn't call you Christina. I know how you hate that.'*"

Mia screamed with appropriate levels of horror. "No one should get called something they don't want to be called. I'll bet your aunt liked it better because it sounds like a girl's name."

"Exactly." It wasn't that I used the name Chris because

it could be for a boy. But also, I didn't hate that about it. "Chris is my name and that makes it a girl's name."

"I was wondering that, actually," said Mia. "So you're a girl?"

"As far as I know. I mean, maybe I'll find out different someday, but I'm pretty sure. You?"

"Yeah, I think I'm a girl too. For a couple of weeks, I tried calling myself *he* in my head, just to see, and it was weird and awkward. *They* was a little better, but still not right. But when I started calling myself *she* again, something somewhere made a little green check and I felt like the word matched me and I matched the word."

"Cool." It really was. I felt cooler just knowing someone who had thought about their gender so carefully.

"I used to be sad that my name didn't shorten to a more gender-neutral name, like yours does. One summer, I went around telling everyone my name was Asher."

"OMG! Asher is one of my favorite names!"

"But not everyone would do it, and that was more disappointing than just hearing my name."

Mia wasn't just cool. She was thoughtful too. "I never asked someone their gender before, you know."

"It's a good habit," said Mia.

"I know, but I was a little nervous about it. I'm gonna try to do it more often, though. Either it'll make someone feel good or it'll remind them to think about how easy it is for them."

I was so proud of myself for having invited Mia to come and sit with me. This was already the longest conversation we'd had, and it wasn't over yet. In fact, Mia opened up a whole new topic.

"So, how's your mom doing?"

"Do you want the good news or the bad news?"

"Both."

I shook my head with fake exasperation. "Of course I'll tell you both. I meant which did you want to hear first?"

"Oh," said Mia. "Why don't you pick?"

"Okay, well, I guess I have to start with the good news, because the good news is that it's been almost a month since her surgery."

"Nice!"

"Buuuuut," I said, "that means we're going home in about two weeks."

"Nooooo!!!!" Mia cried, and I joined her, like two preteen wolves.

"I only met you, like, two weeks ago," I bemoaned.

"Well, I'm just going to have to enjoy you as much as possible until you disappear!" Mia proclaimed.

I climbed off my branch perch, taking my book with me, stepped around the sock stickers as best I could, and into Mia's arms. Mia's hugs felt like home.

The next week went about the same. Reading books, a trip to the library for more books, and ignoring Becca as much as possible. Short conversations with Mom, who was still in a lot of pain after surgery, and often no conversation at all with Vicky, who seemed to be more interested in her theater friends than me. It was hard to say which was worse—how much Becca wanted my attention or how little Vicky did.

Vicky and I weren't texting very much, and when we

did, she didn't say more than a few sentences. She definitely didn't remember the rule that I'm not allowed my tablet between lunch and dinner. Sometimes I would text her in the evening and she wouldn't get back to me until the next afternoon, so I wouldn't be able to text back until that evening. I don't really know what we would have talked about anyway. She wasn't doing GS72BC anymore, and I didn't really want to hear more about her and her YETT friends.

The one bright spot in my days was Mia. We talked every day. I sat on my creek log, even though I picked up dozens of sock stickers, and she sat on her rock, and we talked about everything. We talked about the books we were reading and the disappointment of a book not being as good as its description. We talked about being from the city—Mia was from Boston—and how weird it was not to hear traffic, not even in the daytime. We talked about not being able to reach our best friends—Mia's best friend was on a trip to visit family in India that summer, and even when she could get online, she was awake when it was the middle of the night here. And we talked about our grandparents' weird rules about electronics. Mia was allowed her tablet even less than Becca and I were.

"Yeah, I'm allowed thirty minutes in the morning and thirty minutes at night, plus sixty minutes of television time, and I have to ask permission beforehand," Mia exclaimed.

"Whoa! Sixty minutes isn't even long enough for a movie!"

"That's what I said, and she said I could trade in my tablet time or split the movie over two days."

I gave an exasperated sigh that I hoped expressed the ridiculousness of Mia's grandmother's rules.

"Spending all day with my grandma is pretty boring. All she wants to do is show me her postcard collection and ask if I want to learn to knit, which I don't. But it's not all bad. I get to see you every day!" Mia smiled. "And it could be worse. At least my little brother's not here."

"Don't even get me started!" I said. And then I proceeded to complain how Becca was always talking to me and trying to get me to play with her, when she wasn't pounding her soccer ball against some hard surface.

"Someone gave my brother a kazoo last year," said Mia, "and he played it all the time. I don't know why my mom didn't ever take it away from him."

"Ugh. Same. There was a month when Becca wouldn't talk without the kazoo in her mouth, and if you didn't understand her, she would just say it again louder. Finally the kazoo broke. Under mysterious conditions." I shrugged innocently.

"That's what happened with my brother's too!" We shared a devious smile.

"So yeah, it's nice not to have my brother here," said Mia. "I like to spend a lot of time alone."

"Me too."

"But then . . ." Mia sighed.

"Yeah." I sighed too. "There's a difference between being alone when you want to be alone and being alone when you want to be around someone. Sometimes being alone is the most special feeling in the world . . ."

"And sometimes it's lonely," Mia finished my thought. "Sometimes it's nice to be around someone."

We sat quietly for a bit, listening to the water burble and the birds chirp. It felt comforting to spend time together, even when we weren't talking about anything in particular. Even when we weren't talking at all. It was just good to know that there was someone whose company I enjoyed, and who enjoyed mine.

CHAPTER 15

Nana, Papa, and I were on the porch, drinking lemonade and reading. The air was hot, and the sunshine was creeping toward us, but for the moment, we were in the shade, and things were about as cool and peaceful as they ever got. Becca had even stopped practicing kicking her new soccer ball with its brain-hacking *thump thump thump* that had been making me reread the same paragraph about fourteen times.

It was lovely for about ten minutes, until Becca appeared from out of nowhere.

"I'm bored," she announced.

"Why don't you ram your soccer ball into the side of the house some more," I said dryly. "You might not have left a permanent dent."

"Chris!" Nana admonished me. "Be nice. Becca, I'm glad you've been practicing so hard."

"Why don't you two go down to the stream?" Papa added.

"Yaay!" Becca cheered while I asked, "Do we have to?"

"No," said Nana, with a lie in her voice that meant that we absolutely did have to. "I'm sure there's some unpleasant chore that Papa can assign you."

"Sure is! It's time to mow the lawn," said Papa, looking my way. He'd showed me once how he pushed the manual machine around. It was quiet, and it wasn't too heavy, but it got stuck easily and, worse, most of the lawn was baking in the sun.

Papa turned to Becca, who was too small to push the mower. "And there's fertilizer to be spread."

"Not fair." Becca put her fists on her hips in protest. "I'm not the one who doesn't want to go on a walk! Besides, that stuff smells like *poo*!"

"That's because it *is* poo," I said.

"And if you finish with that," added Nana, "it's dusting day!" She flashed an over-the-top smile and a pair of jazz hands.

Dusting was my hands-down least favorite chore. When you did the dishes or laundry, you got clean dishes or clothes. When you scrubbed the sink, at least it looked shiny after. But dusting was about going into the nooks and crannies that nobody ever looked at and getting rid of the dust so that it became . . . well, pretty much the same as before.

I gave in. "Fine, I'll take Becca on a walk with me. Just let me finish this paragraph."

"Yay!" Becca cheered. "Let's go!" She ran to the beginning of the path down to the stream, which was as far as she was allowed to go on her own, and bounced around from tree to tree until I put down my book and joined her.

It felt kind of weird walking to the stream without a book in hand. I wondered whether we would see Mia.

"Are you gonna show me where you read?" Becca asked.

"Sure," I said.

"And where Mia lives?"

"Sure."

"And where you met her?"

"I met her at the place where I read, so yeah, I think we've got that covered."

Becca ran ahead of me as often as she fell behind while we walked. "Did you see those flowers?" she asked. "How tall do you think that tree is? Have you ever seen a bug like this?"

I didn't bother answering her questions, but she didn't seem to mind. She had already moved on to the next curiosity.

I stopped when we reached the tree Mia and I hung out on, and waited for Becca to notice. She came running back and gasped, like we were witnessing the place where my favorite singer, Miss Kris, had performed her first concert.

"Is this it?"

"Yup!"

"Lucky. And Mia meets you here?"

"Yeah, her grandma lives down that way." I pointed farther down the path that ran along the creek.

"And you sit on that tree together and read?" Becca looked amazed at the heavy log that had fallen across the creek—my own personal perch.

"Well, Mia sits on this stone over here." I gestured at the large, turtle-like rock on the shore. "But yeah."

"Cool." Becca peered out at the water, but she didn't ask about climbing onto the log, and I didn't offer. Maybe she was scared.

After a few minutes of taking in the scene quietly, Becca turned to me abruptly. "Okay, now show me Mia's place!" she said, then shot down the path.

Nana and Papa said I had to go on a walk with Becca, but neither of them said I had to run with her, so I strolled at my own pace until Becca finally turned around and came back my way. Then she looped behind me and ran off again. I didn't think I'd ever had that much energy, not even when I was a really little kid.

I didn't know how she managed to run so fast without tripping on any of the tree roots in the path. Maybe it was a soccer thing. But I did know she ran ahead and then came back to find me about a dozen times.

We reached the last house on the path before it narrowed and headed off into the woods. It was a white two-story home, with a porch way bigger than Nana and Papa's wrapping around three sides of it.

"That's Mia's house?" Becca asked.

"Well, she sure doesn't live at Nana and Papa's!"

"I'll bet you wish she did."

I thought about it for a moment, even though the question had come from Becca.

"Nah," I said proudly. "If she were at Nana and Papa's, it wouldn't be special when I saw her."

Becca stared at the white house a little longer, then yelled, "Race you home!"

"You'll win," I called half-heartedly after her as she took off.

Becca and I were in our room after dinner, soaking in a little electronics time. I was dealing with an especially challenging lemon meringue recipe in *BakeItLast* and Becca was playing some dumb game that made a lady keep screaming as if she were falling off a cliff. When I looked at the screen, I found she was just a lady who didn't like the outfit Becca had picked for her. The lady wasn't wrong, but the screaming was a bit much.

Frank was supposed to pick us up on Saturday. We had made it! Once I was back in town, I could see Vicky in person, and we could get down to GS72BC business. The only bad part was that I would miss Mia, but we had promised to keep in touch.

Papa knocked on the door and popped in his head to say, "Your mom's on the phone."

Becca threw her tablet—onto her pillow, luckily—and ran, yelling, "I wanna talk to Mommy first!"

Fine by me. I had the self-control to go second. When I got to the living room, Mom was on Nana's tiny phone screen, smiling at Becca's story about her latest soccer drill achievement. But my eyes were on Nana, who looked a little pale and unfocused. Papa was quiet too, even though he usually goaded Becca on, especially when we were on a call with Mom. As for Mom—if anything, she looked more tired now than she had when we'd left. She smiled when I told her about my latest read, but it looked like she was smiling mostly because it would hurt to change her face. Something was definitely not right.

Once we got off the phone, we found out what it was.

Well, sort of.

"Before you run off—" said Nana.

Becca had already bounced out of her chair, and I was moments behind her. I had an electronic lemon meringue to perfect. We both turned to look at her. Her face was somber. So was Papa's. Becca sat back down.

"Steve?" Nana gestured at Papa, who let out a slow breath before speaking.

"You see, your mom's recovery isn't going *exactly* as expected." Papa looked over at Nana, who gave a slight shake of her head while staring at her shoes.

I wished I knew what that meant. And so I asked, "What does that mean?"

"Well," Papa continued, "it means that you won't exactly be going home on Saturday."

"Why didn't Mommy tell us herself?" Becca asked,

which was terribly annoying because it was, in fact, a rather good question.

I just yelled "What!" in a way that wasn't a question at all.

"She's feeling very tired," said Nana. "The doctor said that a few more weeks should really do the trick."

"How many more weeks?" I said.

"Just four," Papa said, trying to put a smile on his face.

"But there are only four weeks left in summer!" said Becca.

"What will the next four weeks do that the last six haven't?" I asked.

Papa looked over at Nana as though he either didn't have an answer, or he had an answer he didn't want to tell us.

"The doctor recommended it," said Nana firmly, "and we're going to hope for the best."

People said that a lot about my mom's neck and back: to hope for the best. Mom said it was better to be aware of where she was, and that it was more important to know what she couldn't do now than to hope to be able to do it again someday. I thought she was right.

"I do have one piece of good news," said Papa, holding up a page from the local newspaper. "There's a soccer expo in Greenfield this weekend."

"A soccer expo!" yelled Becca. "Why didn't you tell me?"

"Well, I'm telling you now." Papa winked, as if we hadn't just jumped from a heavy conversation. "You were going to be heading home that day, and I didn't want you to be disappointed that you couldn't go."

"Do you even know what a soccer expo is?" I asked.

"I know what *soccer* is." Becca put her hands on her hips. "And *expo* sounds like it's for *experts*."

Papa laughed. "And beginners too. There will be lots of people, soccer groups, and even a full-length demo game with some professional players."

"And all four of us are going!" said Nana.

Great. Not only were we going to be here and away from Mom for another four weeks, but now I was going to have to spend an entire day with lots of soccer fans, with the bonus highlight of watching an entire sportsball match.

At least I had another whole month with Mia. She

screamed with glee when I told her. And then, of course, she said it was normal to be worried about my mom and that she would be there to talk to.

As for Vicky... well, all I got was a sad face emoji. She didn't even use one of the crying ones. And it was an hour before she added *hope your mom will be okay*.

CHAPTER 16

"Okay, girls, time to go!"

I hated when Nana called Becca and me *girls*. Not because we weren't girls (as far as we knew). But I hated the assumption, and I hated being talked about as if my gender was what was important about me.

"You're not bringing that into the expo," said Papa, pointing at the book in my hand. Everyone knew I got sick if I read more than a road sign while the car was in motion, so I didn't even try to claim it was for the drive.

"But it's a *soccer* expo," I said with a little more whine in my voice than I probably should have. Why would I want to walk around a bunch of tents selling soccer gear and giving out information about local soccer clubs? Why would Nana and Papa even think I might find that anything less than completely misery inducing?

"There's going to be food and music, and we're all going to watch the game together," Nana said, answering my unspoken questions.

"It's just not fair. Soccer is Becca's thing. You wouldn't make her come to a day about reading."

"If there were a book fair nearby while you were here, we would most certainly all go to it," Nana replied. "This is an exciting day for Becca, and I wish you could appreciate that. Besides, Becca's been having a hard time this summer. You get to see Mia just about every day. Let her have this."

There wasn't anything I could say to counter that. So I resigned myself to the lost reading time. It's not like Vicky was doing GS72BC anymore. It was hard to be sure because we hadn't really chatted in over a week. She wrote me a line every once in a while, but mostly it was about how she didn't have time to chat.

We all got into Nana and Papa's car, where Becca was more annoying than usual about patrolling her side of the back seat. Not for the first time, I imagined that if I ever met a genie who could grant me three wishes, the first would be the ability to read in the car. The second would be for a giant ice cream cone. And the third, of course, would be for infinite wishes. Or if that wasn't allowed, infinite genies.

Half an hour later, we pulled into a giant gravel parking lot and followed people in orange hats who directed us to park directly next to the car ahead of us, forming a line of cars filled with soccer fans—and me. Once we got out of the car, we put on our sunscreen and walked all the way down the row. We passed lots of minivans with bumper stickers for the names of local soccer teams and those stick figure stickers who are supposed to represent the mom, dad, two sisters, one brother, and two dogs or whatever that made up the family. These were the kind of people who were going to be at the expo.

It was already hot, and just the walk from the car had me sweating. As some sort of extra rudeness from the universe, just as we reached the end of the row, the orange-hatted people directed the cars to start a new lane right where we were standing. Talk about unfair. I asked Papa why we couldn't just pick our parking spots ourselves, and he said something about crowd control. So now we were part of a crowd that was being controlled. What a fun time.

The expo was free to get into, but we had to wait in line

for wristbands with bar codes on them for some reason. Papa said it was so they could keep track of who had already gotten giveaways from different tents and that I could take my attitude and stick it in my back pocket.

Becca went up to every tent to see if they had something to give away, even if they obviously didn't, like the local teams with nothing on their table but a sign-up sheet and a pencil, with someone smiling way too hard sitting in a small white folding chair, hoping someone would come by and ask about Franklin County's adult amateur soccer league. By the time Becca was done, her shirt was covered in stickers, her arms were covered in wristbands, and her pockets were filled with pencils and erasers. The only good thing was that she found all the places with candy and always brought a piece back for me.

Once we passed through the lane of tents, it was time to take our seats for the game. And if you think a soccer game is boring on a small screen, just imagine the same thing but bigger, sweatier, and without an announcer telling you what's happening. Becca yelled every time the ball changed direction, and Nana and Papa cheered whenever the ball got near the goalies. Me, I read the leaflets other people had left around about healing balms for sore muscles and the importance of the right cleats.

Lots of families wandered in and out of the game, but we stayed for the entire thing. In the heat. In the sun. It was probably over ninety degrees, the official temperature of melting children. The only decent part of the day was when Nana and I took a break to buy some hot dogs and drinks to bring back to the stands. Once I was done with my soda, I had ice cubes to suck on. Becca rubbed hers all over her face and arms to cool off, but I didn't want to make my skin all sticky.

After the game ended (I couldn't tell you the score), we had to walk through Tentland again, and Becca stopped at a bunch of them to see if they had anything new, which of course they didn't, but a few places gave her more stickers to take home.

Papa set up grilling burgers outside when we got back, because apparently a day in the broiling hot sunshine should be followed up by an evening in the still-pretty-hot shade. I grabbed a graphic novel about a kid who joined a roller derby club and sat on the porch. Sports were for reading, not sweating. Becca was kicking her soccer ball, thankfully in quiet circles around the yard instead of against the wall of the house.

It wasn't long before Nana called me in to bring out a big bowl of salad.

"Looks great," said Papa, pointing at the salad with his chin. "On your next trip, can you bring me a plate? The burgers are just about ready to come off. And bring out the buns too, to toast."

"Why doesn't Becca have to help set the table?"

"Oh, let her be. Can't you see she's trying out some of the moves she saw on the field today?"

"Yeah," said Becca. "Let me be."

"But it's not fair! I had to spend the whole day doing Becca's thing, and now I'm supposed to set the table all by myself?"

"Chris, you've been a sourpuss all day."

I've been a sourpuss?! "We spent all day doing her thing and *I'm* the sourpuss?!"

Papa looked at me like he was letting my words ricochet off him and back into me. But I was steeled to deflect and aim them at Becca. Becca was an easy outlet for my frustration on any day, but after a day of being in the sun because she liked to run around after a black-and-white sphere, that was enough to make her a full-on lightning rod.

"I have spent the entire summer here, listening to her kick that stupid soccer ball, and I haven't given you any trouble. I just go out for the day and come home again. She's the one constantly whining that it's hot and that she has no friends here."

That was enough to bring Becca storming over. "It IS hot, especially if you play sports like I do, instead of just sitting around reading. And it's not fair that *you're* the one who made a friend here."

"What's *that* supposed to mean?" I stood up tall to do my best impression of towering over her. I was still taller than her, but not as much as I wanted to be, and clearly not for long.

"You're used to not having friends. You're unpopular,

and everyone knows it. Even Nana and Papa. It's not so hard for you! But me? I need friends!" Then she stormed into the house.

Becca was even dramatic in the way she ended a fight. She was the one who said mean things to me. If anything, I should have been the one to storm off. Instead, Nana brought Becca's dinner inside and watched a dumb little-kid movie with her.

The only thing she said to me about it was that I was older and I should know better. I hated when adults said that. I *did* know better most of the time, but sometimes Becca was just impossible. When she was impossible to grown-ups, they made her stop. But when she was impossible to me, I was the one who was supposed to deal with it.

CHAPTER 17

Becca was still mad at me the next morning, or maybe she was just mad, because she wasn't just kicking the ball into the concrete, she was speed kicking it. Over and over. *Bam. Bam. Bam.* As hard as she could.

Or rather, almost as hard as she could, because when I went up to the sidewalk to get the Sunday paper, she started kicking even harder. *BANG! BANG! BANG!*

I was almost to the curb, with the *BANG! BANG! BANG!* still happening behind me. And then *WHAM!!* The soccer ball hit me on the back of my leg. I almost fell down, it hurt so bad—a bright, hot, stinging pain that left my skin red. The soccer ball bounced off my leg and against the curb. I grabbed it and ran to the end of the block before Becca could stop me.

"Sorry!" Becca cried, running after me. "Sorry! Sorry! Sorry!"

I put the soccer ball down, then looked her right in the eye as I kicked it directly into the open gutter and listened as it bounced and echoed below, joining years' worth of kids' lost balls and leaves and other trash.

Then I limped inside and got some ice for my leg while Becca screamed her side of the story at Nana and Papa.

In an unparalleled show of unfairness, my punishment for having been bruised with a soccer ball was that I had to pay for Becca to buy a new one. As in, we had to drive to the sports store in Amherst that day.

And in a case of double punishment, Becca kicked her new sparkling pink-and-purple soccer ball even more than she did the old one, which I hadn't even realized was possible. The constant *thump thump thump* reminded me of a creepy Edgar Allan Poe story that our English teacher had read us on Halloween last year, where this guy was haunted by a mysterious *thumping* noise under his floorboards that turned out to be a beating heart. It was right in the title of the story, *The Tell-Tale Heart*. The *thumping* that was haunting me was no real mystery either, but that didn't make it any less horrible.

I grabbed the top book off my library stack without even checking what it was and ran down to the creek to wait for Mia. Luckily, it wasn't long before she arrived.

"MIA!" I yelled, joining her on the path. I was too angry to sit. This was a walking conversation.

"CHRIS!" Mia yelled.

"What?" I asked.

"I dunno." Mia shrugged with a grin. "I just thought that's what we were doing."

Mia had known me less than a month and she already knew just when I needed a little laugh.

"No, but really, though." I was back to yelling.

"But really what?"

I told Mia about Becca's soccer ball. About how she had been impossibly annoying all summer, how she had kicked the ball right into my leg, and about how I had to replace it with my own money.

I waited for Mia to agree with me that Becca was terrible, like we always did. Team Little Siblings Are the Worst forever. But she just kind of looked at me.

"What?" I asked.

"Sounds like she hit you with the ball by accident." Mia sounded surprisingly matter-of-fact.

"Well, yeah. Her aim's not *that* good," I said.

"But you kicked her ball down the drain on purpose."

"I guess, but she's been annoying me with that stupid soccer ball all summer! What if it was your brother?"

"I mean, I've never ruined his stuff," said Mia. "And if I did, my mom would probably make me replace it."

"What about that time your brother messed up all those books you organized?"

"He had to spend hours helping me put them back in order."

"Oh." I felt small.

"I mean, I get it!" said Mia. "I've wanted to throw some of his toys off the roof of a tall building just to watch them smash. And if he were here this summer, I just might."

"It is harder without Mom around," I admitted.

"Of course it is," said Mia. "So you lost it for a second and kicked her soccer ball into the drain."

"I did." Somehow saying it made it a little easier to breathe.

"And you bought her a new one, so it's not the end of the world," said Mia.

"I did."

"And I'll bet in the moment you were doing it, it was tons of fun!" Mia beamed.

"It was!"

By the time we had reached the house where Mia dropped off lunch for her grandmother's friend, I felt a lot better. Mia had to go inside and be polite for a few minutes, but then she was back.

"You know what I've been thinking about lately?" Mia asked.

"What?"

"Middle school."

"I was just thinking about that last night!" I exclaimed. "I mean, I'm excited about changing classes, but what if I forget what order to go to them in and end up in the wrong math class?"

"No kidding! And keeping track of all that homework? My older cousin said sometimes three different teachers would assign tests on the same day and there was nothing you could do about it."

I had seen that happen in a sitcom once, and the

kid ended up pulling an all-nighter to study and slept through all three tests.

"But that's not the scariest part," said Mia.

"No kidding."

"The scariest part is, without question, other middle schoolers," said Mia. "There are four elementary schools that all send kids to the same middle school. There are going to be so many new kids!"

Vicky and I had spent hours this spring worrying about how we would manage as new fish in a giant school, but that wasn't my fear anymore. "Actually, I was thinking about the ones I already know. Well, one in specific."

"Vicky?" Mia asked.

I nodded. "We've always done everything together. Neither of us has ever been popular, or even had a whole lot of friends, but that's always been okay. Middle school was going to be fine, because we were going to have each other. Even if we didn't have all the same classes, we would find each other throughout the day, even if it was just for a hug in the hallway. But if I don't have Vicky, I don't know what I'll do."

I burst into tears. Mia massaged my back, but I still felt alone. Mia wouldn't be coming to middle school with me. But she held my hand and walked with me as we talked about how we hoped our middle school libraries would be awesome and maybe let us hang out there during lunch periods.

I heard Becca's new soccer ball pounding before I saw her in the driveway, and I realized that Mia had left the main path to walk up to Nana and Papa's with me.

"I gotta go!" Mia said suddenly, and our conversation dropped mid-sentence. I don't think she realized she had left the main path either.

And then Becca was waving hi at me and asking me whether I had just been walking with Mia and whether she could show me how long she could balance a soccer ball on her shoulder.

That evening, when I tried to call Vicky, I couldn't get through. Again. I tried three times, but it just kept ringing. That meant her tablet had power; she just wasn't answering it. What else could she possibly be doing?

Even if she were reading a book, she could at least message me to tell me she'd call me back at the end of the chapter. That's what we did. Instead, I just stared at the picture of her holding a book up to her face so that all you could see was her eyes until my tablet said *no answer* again.

CHAPTER 18

A few days later, I was sitting on the porch. I had paused for a minute between chapters to imagine what it would be like to fly, which the main character in *Faith: Taking Flight* got the power to do, when Becca's shadow appeared over my book.

"Chris? Could we go on a walk?"

My first instinct was to say *no way on Earth*, but then Becca whispered, "I want to ask you something, but I don't want *them* to hear." She tossed her head in the direction of Nana and Papa, who were in the garden, putting up a new trellis for the beans to climb on.

"Why don't you whisper it to me here?"

"If they see us talking, they'll know something's up," Becca said.

I couldn't argue with that.

"C'mon," she went on, "you owe me for kicking my soccer ball down the drain."

"I replaced it! Besides, you hit me in the back of the leg."

"It was a mistake! I told you I was sorry."

"Okay, fine. What is it?"

Becca lowered her voice more. "I think I heard something important, but I'm not sure what it is."

"Then how do you know it was important?"

"Because Nana and Papa stopped talking about it the second I came into the room."

She had a point. This was becoming a trend.

"Puh-leeeeease?!" Her voice was back at normal annoying-little-kid volume.

"Okay, okay!" I said. "As long as you stop making that noise."

Becca grinned. "Let's go!"

"Now?"

"Why not? Nana and Papa are busy so they won't even notice we're gone."

I was even between chapters on my book. Either she'd timed it perfectly, which was hard to imagine from her half-baked little brain, or she was incredibly lucky.

"Fine," I huffed, and started walking toward the path behind the house, Becca following me. She kept looking back, as if Nana and Papa were going to appear right behind us. We reached the path and I stopped short.

"Okay," I said, "this better be good. What did you hear?"

"Well, Nana and Papa were talking and they said we might not go home this weekend because Mommy has to have surgery."

"The surgery was more than a month ago!"

"Yeah, but Nana said that Mommy had to get a rebidgin or something."

"What's a rebidgin?"

"I don't know. I thought you would."

"Are you sure that's how it's said?"

"Something like that. I don't remember exactly."

"Why didn't you write it down?"

"I didn't know how to spell it!" Becca yelled at me.

"Something's up."

"That's what I'm trying to say!" Becca threw her hands in the air. Then her body and voice softened. "So you don't know what a rebidgin is either?"

I shook my head. I almost said that I might if she had remembered how to pronounce it correctly, but then I would have had to deal with her being upset about that, so I let it slide.

"What do we do?" Becca asked. Even though she was just my little sister, I was her big sister, and according to Mom and everyone, that meant she looked up to me. Like, for help, not just because she was literally smaller than me.

"I think we need to go to Nana and Papa. They need to tell us what's up. We deserve to know!"

"Yeah!" said Becca, heartened by my words. Maybe kinda ew, but also maybe kinda true. "Mommy may be their kid, but she's our mommy."

We walked back to the house, practically marching in step.

"We need to talk," I said in my most serious voice when we reached the garden.

"Yeah, we need to talk." Becca used her serious voice too, but anything she says really seriously sounds kind of silly, and I could see Nana trying to keep from letting out a laugh. I was glad she didn't because I didn't know whose side I would be on in that one.

We probably should have used the walk back to figure out what we were going to say, but we hadn't, so Becca and I just stared at each other. Maybe I should have been the one to ask, but I didn't want to sound dumb if Becca had misheard the word.

"Everything okay?" Papa asked, dropping his trowel into a pile of dirt and standing up.

"No!" I said. "Everything is *not* okay. Becca heard you."

"What did you hear?" Nana asked Becca.

Becca looked over at me as if I had betrayed her. But she was the one who had heard Nana and Papa originally, so really, it was kind of her question. She turned back to Nana and Papa and asked, sounding innocent as a baby lamb, "What's a rebidgin?"

"A rebidgin?" Papa repeated.

"Yeah," Becca said, sounding more confident now. "A rebidgin. You said Mommy had to have one, and it sounded like a bad thing."

Nana and Papa looked at each other, a spark of connection in their eyes, wondering who was going to speak first.

"Your mom is going to be fine," said Nana.

"Then why won't you tell us what a rebidgin is?" I yelled.

"First, it's called a *revision*," Papa said.

I *knew* she'd been saying it wrong!

"Wait," I said. "A revision in school is a do-over, like when you have to edit something to make it better. Does that mean that Mom has to have another surgery?"

"Well, she's smart," Nana said to Papa.

"What's *that* supposed to mean?" I asked.

Papa sighed before he spoke. "She means yes. Unfortunately, your mom does have to have revision surgery to fix up some minor issues."

"When?" I asked.

"Wednesday."

"That's in three days! And what if Becca hadn't heard you? Were you even going to tell us?"

"Yes," said Nana, but the look in her eyes said *maybe*. "We were just trying to figure out how."

"Well, next time, maybe figure it out before an eight-year-old does," I said.

"Hey!" Becca objected.

"Watch your tone!" said Nana.

Papa just looked at me, though I couldn't say whether it was more with confusion or disappointment. I took the silence as an opportunity to walk off with my book. I had already seen Mia for the day, but it was quiet down by the stream, and better yet, no one there was either lying to me or annoying me, which seemed to be the two main options back at the house.

Dinner was very quiet and both Becca and I said *no thanks* when Nana and Papa suggested an evening movie, even when Nana offered to make kettle corn.

"I wanna call Mommy," said Becca.

"We call your mom every night before bed," said Papa.

"I wanna talk to her now," Becca whined.

"Don't whine!" I said, even though I wanted to talk to Mom too.

"Of course we can call your mom," said Nana. "Let me just text Frank and make sure she's awake."

A few minutes later, all four of us were on a video call with Mom and Frank. Mom was wearing her hard neck brace and propped up with a bunch of pillows.

"I'm sorry," said Mom, before we could even say anything. "I should have told you about the revision myself."

"No," said Papa, "we're sorry. We should have told the kids the day you told us. We just didn't want to worry them."

"We're right here, you know," I said. "And we deserve to know what's going on."

"You're right," said Nana. "You do."

"Is the revision why we're staying longer?" asked Becca.

"Obviously!"

"Chris!" Nana snapped. "Don't be so mean to your sister. And yes, Becca, the revision is why your mom needs more time to rest."

"You know," I said, "it's really kind of silly that we both have to stay here. Becca's the one who makes noise at home. If I came home, I'd be able to help out!"

All four adults gave me disapproving looks. Becca looked at me like she was even madder at me than at Nana and Papa for not telling us about Mom's revision right away.

"We talked about this at the beginning of the summer,"

said Frank. "It's been decided. It's best for your mom if you stay there. You want to help your mom, don't you?"

I nodded. I didn't feel like saying anything else.

We didn't talk for much longer, but Mom said about three more times that she was sorry we hadn't found out earlier, and Nana and Papa said it was their fault for not telling us. Becca just said that she missed Mom and wanted to hug her. I didn't say much of anything at all.

After we hung up with Mom and Frank, I messaged Vicky. She didn't answer, but I ranted to her about Nana and Papa lying to us anyway. I hoped she cared that I was stuck being gone for another month. I hope she didn't see it as an opportunity to spend more time with her new friends instead of me.

CHAPTER 19

The next morning, Papa announced that he was making French toast, so we had to wait until breakfast was ready to eat. Becca was upside down like usual, her bare little feet just reaching the top of the couch, where a normal person's head would go.

"I still can't believe Nana and Papa would lie to us!" I said.

"I can," Becca said, as simply as if we were discussing whether ice cream melts in the sun.

"You *what?*" My head whipped around so fast it took a second for my eyes to refocus.

"They were trying to protect us." Becca shrugged, which looked pretty weird upside down.

"From what?" I did not like where this was going. I especially did not like that it was coming from Becca.

"From worrying about Mommy."

"But we have the right to worry about Mom! She's our *mom*!"

Becca shrugged.

"How can you be so calm about it?" I didn't like the idea that she was more calm about the whole situation than I was.

"Because they were trying to be nice. It wasn't nice, but they wanted to be nice. What I don't understand is"—Becca's voice went from calm to eerily quiet—"why did you lie too?"

I was afraid to ask what she was talking about. But I was also afraid not to ask, because it would say that I already knew. Becca just looked at me, still upside down. Her face looked like Mom's when she was disappointed in me. My little sister was disappointed in me. And worse, she was right. I *had* lied.

"You *knew* I was lonely too!" she said.

I didn't say anything.

"And I was here the whole time."

I didn't know what to say.

"I'm right, aren't I?"

I nodded.

Becca's eyes went big.

And that's when Papa called us all to breakfast.

PART III

CHAPTER 20

Before we go any further, I have to tell you something.

Mia Yaring isn't real.
    I made her up.
    Like little kids with imaginary friends.
    Except I'm eleven.
    M-i-a-y-a-r-i-n-g
    is
    I-m-a-g-i-n-a-r-y.

Now you know. And so did Becca.

CHAPTER 21

"Don't tell Nana and Papa!" I begged.

"Why wouldn't I?" Becca stuck her chin out. "You've been mean to me all summer, and you made me feel bad that you made a friend and I didn't, but really, you were just lying to me. You lied to all of us!" She threw up her hands.

"Let me tell them first!"

"You told Mommy she should let you come home and leave me here!"

"Please!"

"You have five minutes." She sounded like a kidnapper, but instead of holding my secret hostage, she was going to set it free for everyone to know.

"Come on, you two," Nana said, poking her head in from the kitchen. "Time to eat!"

A mound of French toast sat at the center of the table, surrounded by syrup, butter, whipped cream, and peach slices. Normally I would have been excited, especially for the peaches, but right then, my stomach felt like cement.

Nana came to the table with a pot of coffee and two mugs, followed by Papa with orange juice—a glass for me, and a plastic cup for Becca. Becca wasn't even old enough to use a regular glass, but she had figured out that Mia wasn't real. How embarrassing.

Worse, she wore an untrustworthy grin that said that I might not even get the five minutes she promised me. If I had been a different kind of person, maybe I would have spoken up immediately. But if I had been a different kind of person, I probably wouldn't have invented an imaginary friend. I thought to myself that Mia would have said something, and then I felt really stupid. I was still pretending.

Becca waited until everyone had been served and had started eating. Well, everyone but me. I managed to load a slice of French toast with the works, but the idea of taking a bite was more than my stomach could bear.

"You okay?" asked Nana when she noticed that my French toast was still a complete square.

I eked out a tiny "Yeah."

"Chris has something to tell you," said Becca, in a perfectly innocent, helpful voice.

I gave her a glare.

"We're all ears!" said Papa.

Nana's smile was both genuine and discomforting.

"It's about Mia," Becca added.

"Well . . ." I took a long pause.

Becca *ahemed* pointedly. The glare in her eyes said that if I didn't fess up, and fast, she was going to say it herself.

"Miadoesn'treallyexist."

"One more time now?" Nana asked.

Apparently, I was supposed to use spaces between the words. I went a step further and made each word its own sentence. "There. Isn't. Really. A. Mia."

"Oh!" said Papa, in surprised relief. "Like Casey Jo!"

I wanted to melt into my chair.

"Wait!" said Becca. "Who's Casey Jo?"

"Casey Jo was your big sister's imaginary best friend," said Papa. "Right around the time you were born, if I remember correctly. She was so excited to have a baby sister and best friend. When you came out like a raisin she couldn't play with, well, she was disappointed."

Forget melting into my chair. I wanted to turn into vapor and disappear into the atmosphere.

"Do we have to talk about this with Becca around?" I asked.

"I want to be around!"

"There's nothing to be ashamed of," said Nana.

But there was everything to be ashamed of. Nana had turned to Becca and was asking whether she'd ever chatted with one of her dolls or stuffed toys. Vapor wasn't going to do it. I wanted to be hurled into the sun and reduced to helium atoms.

"Sure!" said Becca. "I used to tell Bernie Bear my secrets, back when I didn't have friends to talk to."

"I have friends!" I yelled.

"Friend," Becca retorted. "It's just Vicky. Mia doesn't count."

Ouch. Vicky. That meant I had maybe zero friends. "Yeah, well, you'd make friends with a toaster if you spoke heating coil."

"You know what?" said Nana. "I think that's enough of this conversation for the moment."

"Can I be excused?" I asked.

"You haven't touched your breakfast," said Papa. He sounded slightly hurt, but I couldn't tell whether it was real or whether it was the kind of act adults put on when they were trying to give a kid a hard time.

"I'm not hungry," I mumbled. At least that wasn't a lie.

"Oh, let her go," Nana said to Papa.

Ugh. I went to the bedroom I shared with Becca and collapsed onto my bed, my arms over my head, trying to disappear. I had known Mia didn't exist. Not really. But I also knew it was nice to talk to her as if she did.

If I tried hard enough, could I make myself imaginary?

I didn't say anything to Becca all day. She didn't say anything to me either. Normally, I didn't talk to her on purpose, but that day, I went out of my way to make sure I didn't speak near her in case she thought it was meant for her.

I didn't go down to the stream. I didn't want to find

out that Mia wouldn't be there. I couldn't focus to read. I just sat on the porch and stared at the grass. Grass didn't have to worry about imaginary friends *or* real sisters. It just sat there and occasionally let the breeze give it a lift.

Dinner was quiet. Nana and Papa gave up on us pretty quickly and mostly just talked to each other. We made our call to Mom and no one brought up Mia, but Mom commented that we shouldn't be worried about her surgery revision in the morning and that she would see us in two weeks. Then I felt bad because I had been so busy being embarrassed about Mia that I had forgotten to worry about Mom.

I couldn't stay asleep that night. I kept waking up. Maybe I was having bad dreams, though I didn't remember any of them. All I knew was that I was staring at the ceiling, thinking about Becca in the bunk bed above me. Staring and staring. My eyes wouldn't even close. I wondered, *How do we fall asleep? We do it night after night but nobody knows how it happens.* Maybe some scientists did, but I certainly didn't, because if I did, I wouldn't have been lying awake thinking in circles of where the line was between awake and asleep and how we crossed it every night, even though we couldn't make it happen. It was just something our bodies did for us. Usually.

I had read that if you're awake and in bed you should get out until you're tired again so that your body doesn't start to think of your bed as a place to party, so that was what I did. I went to the kitchen for a cup of apple juice and onto the front porch to think a little.

When I opened the door, there was someone already talking on the porch, sitting in Nana's rocking chair.

I jumped back and spilled a bit of apple juice onto my hand. I laughed with relief when I realized that the person in Nana's chair was, unsurprisingly, Nana. But no one else was there. I wondered who she had been talking to. She gestured to Papa's chair next to her and I sat in it.

"Couldn't sleep?" Nana asked.

"Kept waking up."

"Me too. I was just lying awake in bed, thinking thoughts, so I figured I'd come out here and enjoy the air. Lots going on up here?" She tapped at the side of her brain.

"I guess."

"Good thoughts or bad thoughts?"

"Bad thoughts."

"That makes sense. Good thoughts will keep you from falling sleep. Bad thoughts will keep you from staying asleep."

Nana didn't ask if I wanted to talk about it. If she had, I probably would have said no. So we kept quiet for a few minutes, listening to the crickets.

The words finally tumbled out of my mouth. "I knew she wasn't real. But she made me feel a little less lonely. And I wasn't planning to tell anyone about her, but when Becca started talking about not being able to make friends, I don't know what happened. I just said it. I don't even really know how it started. I mean, at first, I was just talking to myself. Kind of like—" I paused. I didn't want Nana to know I had heard her.

"Kind of like I was doing before you came out here?" Nana asked.

"Yeah, I guess. Do you think I'm crazy?"

"Not in the slightest. And even if you did have a mental

health issue to address, I would love you and care about you just as much." She let that thought hang in the air before continuing. "I think you miss your friend Vicky."

"Yeah." It was a pit in my stomach to admit it, but I had spent plenty of time alone before without inventing an imaginary friend.

Nana eyed the doubt in my response suspiciously, then continued. "Plus your mom just had surgery, and is about to have her revision tomorrow. With emotions, one plus one can be eight. Add in spending a summer away from home, and it seems like you were in need of some comfort."

Sometimes hearing someone else say something makes it truer than saying it yourself. There was an ache inside me that I hadn't realized was so sharp. My tears fell, one after another, pooling under my chin and getting my T-shirt wet.

"I can't believe that *Becca* figured it out first. *Becca!* It's just so embarrassing."

"I can understand that." Nana rubbed my back. "And it wasn't fair of Becca to make you tell us. Though I would consider giving your sister a little more credit than you have been. She's not a baby anymore."

I knew that. She had been a toddler, and then a *big kid*, which I thought was a funny term because it's still littler than most kids. But Nana was also right, which I hated. Becca was going into third grade. I could remember being in third grade. I loved to read and I hated gym class—especially when we had to do *team sports*. In a lot of ways, I wasn't that different now.

"I'm glad you told us, though," Nana went on, "because it means we can talk about it. And first thing's first—let me tell you this. Imaginary friends are not a sign of concern for your mental health. And they're not just for little kids. They're connection experiments."

"Like science experiments?"

Nana chuckled. "I suppose, of a sort. Connection experiments are what I call it when I practice talking with people without worrying about the consequences. Like when you tell yourself a joke, but there's no one else there to hear it, because it's funnier if you say it out loud. It's great for when I'm trying to figure out how I feel about a thing. I'll talk about it and see what feels right. Sometimes the person I'm talking to even gives feedback. They're all my thoughts. I'm just doing it in conversation, especially when I'm up late at night."

That made a lot of sense. Mia felt like someone I could talk to, and someone who could answer my questions, even if she couldn't say anything I didn't already know.

Nana didn't ask me any more questions, which was a relief. My brain was a churning mash of thoughts and emotions. It wasn't just me who talked to people who weren't exactly there. Nana did it too. And her people talked back too.

"Who were you talking to when I came out here?"

"Your mom. I was telling her that it's all going to be okay, but really, I was telling myself that." She stayed quiet so long I wondered whether she had fallen asleep, until she stood with a stretch. "Alright then, I'm heading to bed. Turn off the porch light when you come inside."

I listened to the crickets for a while, until I found myself waking up to the beginnings of daylight. The sky was still so dark I couldn't be sure the light wasn't from streetlamps, except that birds had replaced the crickets, and, of course, the fact that there weren't streetlamps out here in Leverett, Massachusetts. I stumbled inside and up to bed to go mysteriously unconscious for a bit more before the day started.

CHAPTER 22

I woke up to a bowl of oatmeal sitting on the kitchen counter.

"You can put that in the microwave to heat it up," said Papa from the table.

I added cut-up peach bits to the oatmeal once it was hot, and took a seat across from him.

"I told your sister not to wake you. I heard you had a late-night chat with Nana. What time did you finally get to sleep?"

"I dunno." I took a bite. I loved how the oatmeal heated up the peach pieces so they immediately dissolved when I bit into them, filling my mouth with a pop of summer.

"You know your mom's revision is today, right?"

How could I forget? I nodded.

"It's also supposed to rain this afternoon."

"Does that mean we get to stay inside?" I looked hopefully at Papa.

"Yes, but Nana and I already discussed it, and our 'no

electronics in the afternoon' rule is still in effect. Frank has promised to call us as soon as there's news, and we'll call you to the phone."

"Fine, I'll just read books the whole time."

"You could also play with your sister. I know you both like Uno." Papa tried to look as innocent as a man suggesting I play cards with my baby sister possibly could.

"I'll think about it." I didn't plan to think about it. "Maybe I'll take a walk now, before it starts to rain."

"Ah, so you *would* like to go outside! Have fun!" Papa said more cheerily than I was prepared to hear.

I grabbed a book and headed down to the creek. I kind of knew Mia wouldn't show up, but I also hoped I was wrong. Not that she had been real before, but I hadn't been thinking about the fact that she wasn't. Now it was all I could think about. I couldn't even remember what she looked like, if I had ever known. Maybe she just looked like me and I hadn't noticed. I decided to distract myself with my book and see if she would appear that way.

Unfortunately, the book I brought was exceedingly dull. So dull that I couldn't concentrate on it hard enough to stop concentrating on whether I could make Mia appear now that I had said out loud that she didn't exist. While the truth was just in my mind, I could pretend it was what was fake. But not anymore. I even tried closing my eyes and counting backward slowly from one hundred, but she didn't show.

Maybe my imaginary friend's grandmother had just been late that morning making up the basket she delivered to the old man farther up the road, like she was Red Riding Hood or something. Or maybe she heard that I told people she wasn't real and decided to prove her lack of existence to me by disappearing on a day I could really use to talk with a friend.

If Mia wasn't going to appear, I could at least use a decent book to read, so I headed back to the house to get another. This time I would read a few pages in the backyard to confirm it was decent before heading back to the creek.

Becca was in the backyard when I got back, her coloring book on her thigh and a pack of gel pens at her side. She was filling in the dark cave behind a dragon atop a mound of gold in his castle. She had colored the dragon in reds, oranges, and yellows so that it looked like it was aflame, with just a touch of green here and there. It was really good, actually. And before I realized what I was doing, I told her so. "That dragon looks really cool."

"Thanks," said Becca without looking up.

My mouth kept talking to Becca as though she were a real person, not just a little sister. "How did you know?"

"About what?"

"What else? Mia."

"Wellllll." Becca drew out the word until it was annoying, but I did my best not to roll my eyes. I did really want to know how she knew when even Nana and Papa hadn't. "At first, I didn't. It was weird because I didn't see any kids in the neighborhood at all, but I didn't think you'd lie about it. But then I realized that you hadn't let Mia borrow any of your books, and you definitely hadn't borrowed any from her, because all the books you've been reading have been library books."

"Wow!" I said. "I wouldn't have ever thought to look for that."

"I'm not a helpless baby, you know." Becca kept shading

the sky with blues while she talked. "And then, the other day, I heard you coming back from the creek trail, and it sounded like you were talking. So I asked if you had been walking with Mia, and you said yeah, but I didn't see anyone with you and I only heard one voice. At least, that's when I started really thinking about it. And when you asked Mommy to let you come home early, you didn't say anything about Mia. But I wasn't *for-sure* sure until yesterday when you said it."

I knew what I had to say next, and I knew I had to say it quickly, before my brain could get in the way and stop me.

"I'm sorry." It didn't feel nearly as bad to say as I thought it would.

Becca looked at me like she couldn't believe I had said it either.

I went on, "I hadn't realized I'd done it at first, really. I was just talking with myself, and doing a bit of pretending. But then I kept doing it, and when you said something about me not having friends, I just wanted to prove you wrong. I'm sorry."

"But I thought you liked spending time alone."

"I do," I said, and again my mouth kept talking without checking in with me. "But being alone isn't the same as being lonely." I paused, but Becca was waiting for more, and she was right. "And I guess I've been lonely."

"I've been lonely too," said Becca. "I miss my friends."

"Me too. I miss Vicky. And I miss Mom."

"Me too."

We didn't say anything after that, but it was more than we had ever said to each other before. We didn't hug, but we sort of let the tips of our shoes touch.

By midday, it was drizzling outside, in a steady sort of way that said *get used to it*. Nana and Papa were going through their DVDs and deciding which to give away. I didn't know why they needed to keep any of them, since everything was online, but Nana and Papa said that the internet is just a bunch of numbers in a computer and they didn't want to lose their favorite movies just because someone unplugged the wrong cord.

Becca and I were in our room. She lay on the floor coloring while I paged my way through *Pebble and Wren*. I'd read it at least a dozen times before, but it was fun, and it was about all I had the attention for.

"Hey, Chris? Is Mommy still in *revision* surgery?" She pronounced the word carefully.

"It should be over by now."

"Is she gonna call soon?" asked Becca.

"Frank has been sending Nana updates." Updates that said there was nothing to update.

"I want to talk to Mommy."

"She has to wake up from the anesthesia first," I reminded her.

"Oh yeah. So now what do we do?"

"I saw a deck of Uno cards on the game shelf . . ."

"I know how to play Uno!" Becca exclaimed.

"Everyone knows how to play Uno."

"I didn't used to!"

She was right. I remembered trying to teach her when she was four. Even though she knew how to count to ten, she kept getting confused about the rules and then wandered off halfway through a round.

"Tell you what," I said, "if you go get the cards, I'll play a round with you." I didn't think I'd ever seen her move so fast, not even running after a soccer ball.

Once she brought the cards back, I shuffled the deck with a cool arch, like Frank had taught me, and dealt out seven cards each. It didn't take long before I had one card left, and it was a *Wild*, so I went out. Becca only had three cards left in her hand, though, and one of them was a zero, so she only got eleven points. I shuffled again, and this time I let her deal. She beat me with two *Skip* cards still in my hand. I was just getting ready to shuffle for a third round when Papa popped his head into the room.

The grin on his face when he saw that we were playing together said *I told you so*. I would have explained that this was a special circumstance, but Becca spoke first.

"Is Mommy on the phone?" Becca asked with wide eyes.

"As a matter of fact, she is!" Papa gave Becca a high five before she ran out of the room.

That left Papa with me. "She's turning more and more into a human every day," he said, then followed Becca.

When I got to the living room, Frank was telling Nana some story about how hard it was to park in the hospital garage and how ridiculous it was that they expected you to pay for parking on top of everything else.

Becca was bouncing around in front of her. "When are we gonna get to talk to Mommy?"

"Hold your horses!" said Nana.

But Becca was right. Frank could tell her boring, grown-up car story anytime, and I think even Frank realized that, because she finished it with "Well, you know how capitalism is."

Nana laughed. "Okay, the kids are here now, and I think there's someone else we'd all like to see."

"I gotta warn you," said Frank, "she's only been awake post-surgery for a little while, and she's still pretty loopy. But she insisted we call."

I could hear Mom's voice yelling, "For the love of glitter, if you do not hand me my phone right now, I am going to get out of this bed and take it from you."

"She doesn't sound loopy to me at all," I said.

To prove her point, Frank turned the phone to face Mom, who was half-heartedly flailing her hands and not moving any other part of her body. Then Frank turned the camera back on herself with a *do-you-see-what-I-mean* face before giving us Mom again.

We didn't talk for long since Mom was tired, and we didn't really say anything special or important. It was good to know the surgery was over, but I missed seeing her in person, hugging her and letting her kiss me on the forehead even though I thought I was kind of too old for that sort of thing. She blew us kisses and told us a dozen times that she loved us and she was excited to have us back home soon. I didn't have words to tell her how much I missed her and how I couldn't wait until I could snuggle up to her and smell her vanilla shampoo and minty pain-relief cream.

After the call, Becca and I went back to our Uno game. I won, but it was super close: 510 to 495. And if it hadn't been almost dinnertime, we might have played more.

It was amazing how not annoying Becca could be.

CHAPTER 23

The last week at Nana and Papa's was perhaps the weirdest in my life.

Not because of Mom's revision surgery. It was a big deal and had everyone's emotions turned up high, but it wasn't exactly weird. It was just what life was like when you had a mom with chronic pain.

And it wasn't even because it rained every day that week. Rain wasn't all that weird either. In fact, it would have been way worse if it hadn't rained at all that summer, but usually it was either sprinkles in the morning or a quick shower in the afternoon. This was five days of nonstop rain. And again, not weird, except for what ended up happening.

The weird part was how Becca and I interacted that week. As in: We did. If you'd pushed me on it, I might have even said we had fun. We laughed. A lot. I mean, I wouldn't hang out with her at home or anything, but it wasn't as terrible as it could have been.

Weird.

• • •

"Uno!" called Becca, laying a green zero on the discard pile that sat between us on the porch bench. This was the day before we were leaving and it wasn't raining, so Nana and Papa had sent us outside. The ground was wet from the morning, and the sky was still dark and gray, like it could pour again at any moment.

"Again?" I groaned.

Becca grinned and shrugged. Normally I would have found both impossibly annoying, but I had to hand it to her, she had card-slaughtered me when she pulled out a third *Draw Two* to lay on top of the one I'd thought was a fatal blow. Suddenly, I had eight cards in my hand, and none of them matched the discard pile. And now she had one. Worse, we had agreed to play the way where if you don't pick up a card you can use, you have to keep picking up until you do.

"Can't I just pass and let you go out?"

"Nope!" Becca stuck out her lips in a weird, scrunchy sort of face. "I want to see how many cards you have to pick up first."

She was right. It wasn't fair to not let her see how

thoroughly she had destroyed me. I would demand no less of her. A ridiculous ten cards later, including two skips, but in the wrong colors, I finally pulled a blue zero and placed it on top of the green zero, hoping I had stymied her by changing the color.

She laid down another green zero and beamed.

"You had it no matter what!"

"Not totally. You could've gotten a wild card. Or another draw two."

"Yeah, I know the rules of the game."

"If you know the rules so well, how come you keep losing?" Becca raised her eyebrows.

It felt like the kind of sentence that should make me mad, but somehow it didn't.

"I have to do something to help my poor little sister!" I teased back.

Papa walked by, carrying his gardening gloves and tools in a basket. "You two aren't having fun now, are you?"

"No!" Becca and I said in unison. We tried very hard not to giggle, and failed.

"I see how it is," Papa said. "I'm heading out to the

garden to pick a few things before the rain starts up again. Want to join me, Becca?"

"Do I have to?"

"Not if you don't want to."

"No thanks." Becca handed me the messy stack of cards.

Papa looked at Becca and then over at me. "Do you want to come help then? For a little break from you-know-who?"

I straightened the cards into a neat stack and then fanned them out. At least all the cards were facing in the right direction. When Becca collected the cards, there was usually some going the wrong way. Or at least there used to be.

"Actually," I said, "I think I'm gonna stay here. Becca's won three games in a row and it's time for my comeback."

"Suit yourselves," said Papa. Then he added to himself as he headed off to the garden, "It's fine, Steve. Just because no one wants to garden with you doesn't mean they don't love you."

"I love you!" Becca called out.

"Me too!" I added.

"Thank you!" Papa called back, then whistled his way off to the garden. He didn't really want one of us with him so much as he wanted to tease us that we'd rather spend time with each other. Or tease me, I suppose. I was the one who had been ignoring Becca. In favor of someone who didn't even really exist. Maybe Becca wasn't the only one who was difficult sometimes. Ugh.

"Just gimme the cards." I shuffled them and handed them out. Maybe this time I'd win.

And also, maybe, it wasn't all about winning.

Becca had been surprisingly not terrible, but talking with your little sister wasn't the same as chatting with your friend, especially your best friend. Especially when you weren't entirely sure what was up between the two of you. It had been nearly a week since I'd heard from Vicky, and way more than that since we had really talked, so I was excited that there was a message from her when I got my tablet for the evening. And I was even more excited once I read the message. Nervous too, but mostly excited.

Vicky: I'm sorry I've been ignoring you

I stared at it for a while, not sure what to say back. I didn't want to say she hadn't been ignoring me, because she had been.

> Me: you're allowed to have other friends
> Vicky: I know. I'm sorry that I forgot that you're my *best* friend

That felt really good to read. I knew it was true, at least in my brain, but it warmed up that piece of my heart that held Vicky close. And it felt good that Vicky responded right away.

> Me: thanks

Fine, maybe I had something to be sorry about too. Or at least, to share with Vicky.

> Me: can we video?
> Vicky: please

"Okay." I wrung my hands into a ball once we were on screen together. "Here's the thing. So, Mia? The kid I've been hanging out with? She's—well—she doesn't exist."

"What?" Vicky looked surprised more than angry. At least, that was what I hoped she was. I kept talking, partly because I had more to say and partly because I didn't want to find out if I was wrong.

"I was lonely here. And I like being alone, but this was different. I missed you. At first, it was fun just to imagine someone I could wave to as I read my book. But then she started talking to me. Or should I say, *I* started talking to me. And when Becca said something about me not having any friends, I told her and Nana and Papa about Mia. I told them I made a friend, but I didn't tell them I made *up* a friend." I half grinned at my own joke, but I didn't look to see whether Vicky grinned back. "I mean, it was just nice to have someone around who's a lot like me. You know, since I didn't have you. You were hanging out with your new YETT friends all the time and I guess I got jealous because then I was lying to you too."

I sniffled once, twice, and then I was crying. Quietly, but the tears flew down my face. "I'm sorry."

Vicky didn't say anything right away and I got nervous that maybe I had lost my real friend by making up a pretend one.

"Can I tell you something?" She didn't sound mad, at least.

"Always."

"I haven't seen anyone from YETT since the last day of camp."

"Those jerks! They don't know who they're missing!"

Vicky smiled, and I realized her face was wet with tears too.

"And worse," Vicky said, "I didn't even come close to finishing GS72BC because of them! They kept inviting me to pool parties and saying reading is for when you're stuck indoors because it's cold out."

I thought about how much I had read by the creek and on the porch. "I have to disagree. Reading outdoors is fabulous."

"I should have known that they weren't really my kind of people when they said that. I guess I was just lonely."

"Yeah, well, at least your fake friends are real people," I quipped, then got nervous that I had insulted her. But she started laughing.

"Oh good," I said with relief. Mia never disagreed with me, and she had laughed at all my jokes, but that was because I controlled her. It was different, connecting with a real friend. Better. "I missed you, Vicky."

"I missed you too, Chris."

"And I have an idea for how save GS72BC! I know you don't *love* picture books, but my sister has a ton of them, and some of them are pretty good. We get home Monday. School doesn't start until Wednesday. That gives us a whole day. How many books do you have left to read?"

"Like, half of them."

"No problem! Picture books go super fast."

"One request," said Vicky.

"Nothing super sticky sweet. I know you. Clever books only."

"Okay, two things. Can we read outside in my

backyard because reading is a wonderful summer outdoor activity?"

"Ooh! I love that idea!"

It felt good to know Vicky and what kinds of books she liked. But it was even better that Vicky could think of things I didn't.

CHAPTER 24

Becca and I were on the porch, playing Uno again, when Frank pulled into the driveway the next day. We both ran down to give her a big hug.

"I've missed you!" Frank squeezed Becca tight. "And you, my little bookworm, get over here." Frank was small but strong, and she hugged with her whole body. It wasn't as good as seeing Mom, but it was close.

Three of Mom's friends were watching over her while Frank was with us, so Frank was okay with staying for lunch again. Nana made a huge lunch, of course. Ham and mashed sweet potatoes, which were Mom's favorites, and Nana promised that we would be taking home plenty of leftovers. There was also salad and dinner rolls, as well as chocolate pudding pie for dessert.

"This is absolutely amazing," Frank announced. "I haven't eaten this well since the last time I was here."

Nana beamed with pride.

I was worried that Nana or Papa, or worse, Becca, would say something about Mia, but no one did. Maybe I would tell Mom when I got home. Maybe. But if so, I wanted to be the one to do it.

After lunch I was outside, reading as usual, while Frank got the car ready. Nana came out onto the porch with a wrapped package that she laid on the table next to her.

"I'm going to miss you two," she said. "It's going to be real quiet around here tomorrow."

"You could keep Becca," I joked.

Nana laughed. "I know you love her more than you let on. Don't worry. I won't tell anyone."

"I still don't like her."

"I didn't say you did. But you love her."

I didn't say anything.

"You do."

I squirmed in my chair.

"I want to hear you say it."

Fine. "I love her."

"Again. Use her name."

"Mrph-loveBecca." I mumbled it really fast. So fast that I couldn't feel it happening. Nana noticed.

"Once more."

"Why?"

"Sometimes saying things helps make them real."

"What if I don't want it to be real?"

Nana looked me up and down.

I sighed. "Okay, fine. I love my sister, Becca." I felt the words bounce around in my head. They felt weird, out of place. But my brain didn't explode and I didn't break out in hives.

Nana put her hand over mine. "I know."

"That makes one of us."

"That's okay," said Nana. "Sometimes it takes time to adjust to change. Especially when it's the other person changing. I got you something. A bit of a going-home gift." She handed me the package from the table. It was a hard, flat rectangle. A common gift-shape for yours truly.

"Is it a book?"

Nana laughed. "Yes, Holmes, it's a book."

"Is it a good one?"

"I sure hope so. Open it."

It was a book alright. A beautiful, shiny black book with little silver stars. But there was no title. And no author. And inside, there were no words, just blank lines.

"It's a diary," said Nana. "Or a journal, if you prefer. Journaling is a great place to try out your thoughts. Connection experiments, you know. Someone to talk to if you don't want to talk out loud."

"Another experiment?" I asked.

"Yup," said Nana. "Pretty much all of life is an experiment. Trying out one thing, testing another, figuring out what gets you the results you want."

"Sounds like fun." I wasn't convinced.

"It's the greatest fun there is." Nana pulled a pen out of her pocket. "Here. Try it out."

After Nana was out of sight, I opened the cover with a soft crack to the first lightly lined page.

Sept 4

My twelfth summer on the planet is ending. In a week, I'll be in middle school. I remember being a kindergartner lining up in the schoolyard one morning, thinking I would never be as old as those giant fifth graders. And now even Becca is two years away from being one of them. Old people talk about the years flying by, but I didn't think it would start so soon.

As I wrote, I could feel Mia beside me. I didn't dare look up, for fear she would disappear. Instead, I kept writing. And as I did, I felt Mia slide into me, so that we were moving my hand, our hand, together, the words hers as much as they were mine.

I was afraid to stop writing, afraid to change the moment in any way. I turned the page as quickly as I could to get my pen back on the paper. I wrote until my hand cramped and I had to stop for a moment. But when I did, the muscles around my thumb throbbing, I could feel her, still there.

Maybe I didn't make a new friend that summer. But I learned how to *maybe* not dislike my sister so much. And I got a new journal, one that I would spend the rest of the year writing in until I filled up every page with my words and thoughts. With me.

CHAPTER 25

The drive home to Staten Island was a lot like the drive to Massachusetts. At least, the scenery outside was the same. But in the car, it felt different. Instead of three people nervous about how the summer and Mom's surgery would go, we were two and a half months wiser. Frank belted out the same sorts of tunes from the front seat. Becca and I still fought our back-seat border battles, especially when she decided to lay her legs diagonally so that she wasn't technically on my side of the seat, even though her feet were encroaching on my space, but we also laughed together when Frank tried to hit high notes and sounded like a balloon losing air.

I didn't fall asleep on the ride home, and neither did Becca. We were too excited to see Mom. When we got home, she was sitting up in bed, her hard plastic collar around her neck and a giant grin on her face.

Frank reminded Becca not to jump on the bed too hard, and I'm glad she did, because I might have thrown myself right at Mom too. Instead, we took turns with soft hugs.

"I missed you, Mommy!" Becca said. "Can I cuddle with you?"

"If you do it carefully." Mom warned Becca not to make any sudden movements. Becca slowly and gently nestled her way into Mom's side.

They looked so comfortable. If Becca hadn't been a part of it, I would have wanted to join. Then I realized that if Becca hadn't been there, there wouldn't have been an *it* to join. And actually, as long as I snuggled the other side of Mom, I wouldn't be touching Becca directly.

"Can I cuddle too?" I asked.

"Always, sweetie."

I cautiously sat on the bed and scooched my body to Mom's free side. We laid together for a bit. Mom asked us about our summer and Becca told her about the soccer moves she had practiced, and about the soccer expo. She didn't mention that I had kicked her old soccer ball down the drain though. And she didn't mention Mia.

Becca started acting out the moves and Mom reminded

her that she either needed to be still or get out of the bed. Becca gave Mom a kiss on the forehead and then bounded off to check on her room. I kept snuggling.

"What a short attention span that kid has!" said Mom.

"Enh, she's young."

"Excuse me?" Mom's surprise sent the end of her question soaring up in pitch. "Did you, Chris, *my* older daughter, just give Becca, *her* younger sister, an *inch* of latitude? The doctors said that I would continue to feel the effects of the surgery over the coming months, but this is incredible."

"Mom!" I tried to sound annoyed but my laugh gave me away. I squeezed her around the stomach and buried my head against her upper arm. "Am I okay here?"

"Yeah, as long as you don't put any weight on my shoulder. So, I heard all about soccer. I'm assuming your summer was a little different."

"You could say that."

"So, how was it?"

Uhhh. "It was okay. I missed you."

"What did you do?"

Eeep. "I read a lot."

Mom blew a raspberry. "Uh, yeah, I know that. I mean, what else did you do? You didn't read sixteen hours a day, did you?"

"Did Nana tell you?" I asked.

"Did Nana tell me what?"

I wasn't sure whether that meant that Nana hadn't told her, or whether she was just being difficult. If she didn't know, maybe we didn't have to talk about it at all. And maybe we didn't, but I wanted to. Or, well, I didn't want to have to tell her, but I wanted her to know. Everyone else knew, and I liked the idea of keeping the secret from Mom even less than the idea of how it would feel to tell her. Not to mention how much worse it would be if she found out from Becca.

"Well . . ."

"A hole in the ground," Mom replied.

"Ha ha. Can I tell you something embarrassing?"

Mom slowly turned her body to the side so that she was facing me.

"Oh, sweetie, what happened to you?"

"It's not what happened to me. It's more of what I did."

"You can always tell me anything, Chris. Whatever it is, we'll figure it out."

"I think it's already figured out, actually," I said. "Nana and I talked about it."

"My mother is a very smart woman." Mom smiled. "So, what's up?"

"Imadeanimaginaryfriend."

"Excuse me?"

Oops. I'd done it again. Adults liked spaces between the words of awkward admissions. "I made an imaginary friend this summer. Her name was Mia, and I knew she was imaginary the whole time, and I don't really know why I did it, but it was nice to have someone to talk to and read books with."

"That sounds like enough of a why to me," said Mom. "In fact, I have a buddy in my head named Grover."

"Like the monster on *Sesame Street*?"

"Exactly. When I'm in pain, sometimes he screams and flails and does that classic Grover *why does nobody like me?* wail, and it makes me feel a little better and less alone."

"Nana said she talks to imaginary people too. So I guess I'm a third-generation weirdo."

"Connection experiments are a lot more common than you might expect."

"You know about those?"

"Of course! Nana is my mother, remember. I grew up with her. I mean, you're totally a weirdo, just not because you talk to yourself. In fact, I think it might be pretty weird to never chat yourself up. I mean, you're around yourself all the time, right? At some point, it's rude not to strike up a conversation."

Mom gave a goofy grin and let me give her a long hug that only ended when Becca came in declaring that I had been hogging Mom and it was her turn for *undivided attention*. She even came in with a written petition, though she was the only person who signed it, and she spelled it *Undevided Atenshun*.

If it hadn't been my annoying little sister, it would have been funny.

And if I'm really being honest, it *was* funny.

CHAPTER 26

Frank and I sat at the kitchen table eating cereal together. It wasn't waffles or eggs and hash browns or any of the amazing breakfasts we'd had at Nana and Papa's, but we got to eat whenever we wanted. Mom wasn't up yet, and Becca had already eaten and put her dirty dishes in the sink.

"So, last day of summer vacation, hunh?" said Frank, smiling broadly. "You got plans?"

"I was gonna hang out with Vicky."

"Oh!" Her eyes went wide, but she recovered quickly. "Well, it's up to you, I suppose, and you're welcome to invite her, but I was thinking about taking you and Becca to the beach to celebrate making it through this summer."

Becca came running down the hallway, yelling, "I heard that! Can Mommy come?"

"It's going to be a bit too much walking for her, right

now," said Frank. "But we can call her from the beach, and maybe we can find her a seashell to bring home."

Becca sighed, and she wasn't wrong.

"But maybe in the fall we can go minigolfing."

I turned around to see Mom standing with her cane. I ran over to her and hugged her tight. Becca joined in.

"That is, if you don't suffocate me right here and now!" Mom laughed. "Okay, okay, let me sit down."

"Mini-golfing?" Frank looked at Mom, her eyebrows raised with doubt.

"I wouldn't play, but I could walk with you all from hole to hole."

Frank's frown didn't let up.

"What?" Mom cried. "There are benches all over the place. And the doctor said next month I'll be starting physical therapy to strengthen my muscles back up again. They'll want me to walk around."

"We'll see." Frank let go of the topic, but squeezed Mom's hand with both of hers to say that she loved Mom's tenacity as much as anything else about her.

I checked with Vicky, who said that the beach was a perfect outdoor place to read and that she would bring sunglasses in case it got too bright. I spent most of the rest of the morning in Becca's room, picking out the perfect set of picture books to bring. Becca even helped with a few of her favorites.

Normally I was a fan of getting to choose the book to match the reader's mood, but in this case, we had thirty-six picture books to slam out, so Vicky was going to have to read everything I brought. Nothing too sugary sweet, and I made sure not to bring anything with too many words. There were even a few wordless books, which would go super quickly. Vicky would be done in less than an hour and we'd still have plenty of time to spend together at the beach.

Vicky was waiting on the front steps when we pulled up to her house. She ran to the car and attacked me the moment I opened the door, tackling me back into the car with a massive hug.

"Good to see you too, Vicky!" Frank said, and Becca gave her usual, loud "Hi, Vicky!" but Vicky and I were laughing too hard to say anything back.

Finally our laughs settled into the occasional chuckle burst, and we were able to get our seat belts on. Frank joked that she felt like a chauffeur with all three of us squeezed into the back seat, but there was no way Vicky and I were splitting up. Frank said Becca was too little to sit in the front seat, and Becca said that as long as she got a window, she didn't care. So I sat in the middle seat and we headed off to the waves. Frank found a parking spot a couple of blocks from the boardwalk, and with everyone carrying something, we made it to the sand in one trip, even with the two canvas bags I had packed with picture books.

It was the last day before public school started, so there were lots of kids around, but it wasn't as crowded as it could have been. We found a flat patch about halfway up from the water and Frank staked the bright red beach umbrella into the sand. She said it was as much to help us find our way back from the water as it was to provide shade.

By the time Vicky and I spread out our towels and anchored them with our shoes and bags, Becca had already started playing with her soccer ball. She could even bounce the ball on her knee a few times before she had to go running after it. Luckily, balancing the ball on her foot and running around with it in the sand was way quieter than kick drills against Nana and Papa's house.

"Great work!" Vicky said. "And I don't think I've ever seen a pink-and-purple soccer ball before! It's very pretty."

"Thanks," said Becca, getting ready for another attempt. "Chris got it for me."

"Long story," I added.

"Yeah, and we're friends now!"

"Oh really!" Vicky sounded as surprised as I would have been about a month ago.

"I mean, we're not *friends*," I said. "We're sisters."

"But you like me now!"

"I wouldn't go that far. But you're not the worst you've ever been. In fact, there are maybe some things about you that aren't that terrible."

"Thanks!" Becca beamed as though I had given her a genuine compliment. She got five volleys in before the ball went sideways and she ran after it.

"I'm glad you're home," said Vicky.

"I'm glad you're here," I said.

We sat quietly for a little bit.

"I still haven't heard from any of the kids from YETT," said Vicky.

I noticed she didn't call them her friends. "I'm sorry to hear that. If it helps, I haven't heard from Mia either."

Vicky waited for me to start laughing before joining in.

"Whatcha laughing about?" Becca asked.

"Our friends not talking to us," said Vicky.

Becca's forehead wrinkled. "That doesn't sound very funny."

"It isn't," I said.

"Then why are you laughing?"

Vicky put her arm around my shoulder and I put my arm around hers, and like the best friends we were, we spoke as one. "Because we have each other!"

"You two are weird!" said Becca.

"I sure hope so!" I said.

Vicky put her other arm around me and gave a big squeeze. I hugged her back, as tightly as I could, before we settled into our reading positions. Vicky read quickly, and I was right—she was done in way less than an hour. I was also proud that she laughed at the books I thought she would laugh at. Not that I had written them, of course, but I knew my best friend well enough to be able to guess what she would find funny enough to laugh out loud at, even when trying to race through a pile of books.

We celebrated the completion of GS72BC with a giant cheer and a call to Mom, who cheered along with us and asked us for some book recommendations. After we hung up, we ran into the water. Frank and Becca joined us, though Frank went back to the blanket soon after. She said she wanted to make sure nothing got taken, but I think she wanted to take a nap now that we weren't all hanging around on the blanket.

In the water, Vicky showed me some of the theater games she learned at YETT. My favorite was "Mirror, Mirror," where you stood in front of each other, face to face. One person would start moving, and the other would be the mirror, copying all their motions, trying to do them at the exact same time. Usually you did things with your legs and feet too, but we stuck to the halves of our bodies that were above the water.

At YETT, a counselor would announce "switch" and whoever had been the mirror would start moving and the other person would copy. Vicky said that if you got really good at it, you could not say who was the mirror and you would follow each other and it was just all sort of soft and it worked. Vicky said that was an actor's high point—when you were both the mirror.

For a moment, I thought about how good Mia and I would be at this game. We had the same mind, so we could match ourselves perfectly. We could probably both be the mirror right away. But then, maybe because I was distracted, I messed up and assumed Vicky was going to pat herself on the head again, when really, she did a move where she faked me out and bopped me on the head instead. I laughed and tried to bop her back, but she ducked and then headed for the sand.

She barely reached shore before I tackled her and bopped her on the head. Then we were bopping each other and laughing until we could barely breathe, the trails of waves still splashing our legs. Mia could never do that.

But Vicky and I could. And I couldn't wait to journal about it later.

GREAT SUMMER 72 BOOK CHALLENGE: CHRIS'S LOG

You can read most of the books Chris read (the two with asterisks are made up), and you don't have to do it all in one summer.

#	Book
1	*Show Me a Sign* by Ann Clare LeZotte
2	*The Last Mapmaker* by Christina Soontornvat
3	*Prairie Lotus* by Linda Sue Park
4	*Rad Women Worldwide* by Kate Schatz, illust. by Miriam Klein Stahl
5	*Unidentified Suburban Object* by Mike Jung
6	*A Seed in the Sun* by Aida Salazar
7	*Brooms* by Jasmine Walls, illust. by Teo DuVall
8	*Breakout* by Kate Messner
9	**Time Hobo: A Rogue Space Book* by G. Ray

10 *The Girl from the Sea* by Molly Knox Ostertag

11 *Merci Suárez Plays It Cool* by Meg Medina

12 *Written in the Stars* by Aisha Saeed

13 *Tight* by Torrey Maldonado

14 *Answers in the Pages* by David Levithan

15 *Stargazing* by Jen Wang

16 *The Phantom Tollbooth* by Norton Juster

17 *Shooting Kabul* by N.H. Senzai

18 *Super Boba Café* by Nidhi Chanani

19 *Maizy Chen's Last Dance* by Lisa Yee

20 *Class Act* by Jerry Craft

21 *The Lost Girl* by Anne Ursu

22 *Where the Sidewalk Ends* by Shel Silverstein

23 *Those Kids from Fawn Creek* by Erin Entrada Kelly

24 *Dactyl Hill Squad* by Daniel José Older

25 *Elementals: Ice Wolves* by Amie Kaufman

26 *The Girl with the Silver Eyes* by Willo Davis Roberts

27 *Some Places More than Others* by Renée Watson

28 *Attack of the Black Rectangles* by Amy Sarig King

29 *Winnie Nash Is Not Your Sunshine* by Nicole Melleby

30 *Not Your Sidekick* by C.B. Lee

31 *The Order of Things* by Kaija Langley

32 *The One and Only Ivan* by Katherine Applegate

33 *Almost Flying* by Jake Maia Arlow

34 *Splinter & Ash* by Marieke Nijkamp

35 *The Antiracist Kid* by Tiffany Jewell

36 *The Laura Line* by Crystal Allen

37 *Spirit Hunters* by Ellen Oh

38 *Get a Grip, Vivy Cohen!* by Sarah Kapit

39 *Playing the Cards You're Dealt* by Varian Johnson

40 *My Life as an Ice Cream Sandwich* by Ibi Zoboi

41 *The Last Cuentista* by Donna Barba Higuera

42 *Bingo Love* by Tee Franklin, art by Jenn St-Onge, colors by Joy San

43 *As Brave as You* by Jason Reynolds

44 *The Wild Ones* by C. Alexander London

45 *Brown Girl Dreaming* by Jacqueline Woodson

46 *The Marvellers* by Dhonielle Clayton

47 *Roller Girl* by Victoria Jamieson

48 *A Good Kind of Trouble* by Lisa Moore Ramée

49 *Small Town Pride* by Phil Stamper

50 *Elle Campbell Wins Their Weekend* by Ben Kahn

51 *Set Me Free* by Ann Clare LeZotte

52 *Sail Me Away Home* by Ann Clare LeZotte

53 *Sir Callie and the Champions of Helston* by Esme Symes-Smith

54 *Faith: Taking Flight* by Julie Murphy

55 *Finally Seen* by Kelly Yang

56 *Witchlings* by Claribel A. Ortega

57 *Pebble and Wren* by Chris Hallbeck

58 *Lunar Boy* by Jes and Cin Wibowo

59 *Nimona* by ND Stevenson

60 *Pride: The Celebration and the Struggle* by Robin Stevenson

61 *To Night Owl from Dogfish* by Holly Goldberg Sloan and Meg Wolitzer

62 **Swords & Secrets* by B.A. Delacourt

63 *Everlasting Nora* by Marie Miranda Cruz

64 *Enemies* by Svetlana Chmakova

65 *Queer, There, and Everywhere: 27 People Who Changed the World* by Sarah Prager

66 *Tegan and Sara: Junior High* by Tegan Quin, Sara Quin, illust. by Tillie Walden

67 *The Jumbies #1* by Tracey Baptiste
68 *A High Five for Glenn Burke* by Phil Bildner
69 *The True Definition of Neva Beane* by Christine Kendall
70 *Barakah Beats* by Maleeha Siddiqui
71 *Basil and Oregano* by Melissa Capriglione
72 *Different Kinds of Fruit* by Kyle Lukoff

ACKNOWLEDGMENTS

I started writing this book in 2019, and I knew each person could only read it once for the first time. Thanks to my mom, Cobre, Kaija, Sylvie, Lexi, Wendy, Sandhya, Vee, and Phoebe for joining the insiders' club early and for your feedback so that I could make a better book for everyone else. You took one for the literary team. And thanks to Kinsey for the great recommendations to fill out Chris's GS72BC log.

Particular appreciation for Sandhya and her lived experience as a disabled mom. You are *not* a burden. You *have* burdens. And you're not alone. Many thanks to Corrie, who kept the ship moving—thanks for all the dishes. You know exactly which ones I mean. And great fondness for Phoebe, who helps me be the most me I can be. Her like I.

Alicia—you are not A Licia. You *have* Licias. Thank you. Always.

Local bookstores are gifts to our community. Lexi of High Five Books is a gem.

Writers I am lucky to call friends and colleagues: Mike, Ann, Tracey, Hannah, Sarah, Kyle, and so many more my little brain can't handle it! Even if your name isn't here, it's in my heart. And if you write middle grade, maybe in Chris's book log.

My life is endlessly enriched by friends and loved ones, old and new, including Beth, Shahn, Amy, Cobre, Joey, Cal, Lee, Coates, and Reese. Thanks for sharing your lives with me!

Of course, I wouldn't be here without my parents. Thank you to the real Cindy and Steve for supporting my storytelling the whole time. And for putting up with how different Robin and I are. To my sister's kids, Kadyn and Brinley, who get more fabulous each year. And to my little sister Robin—you've turned into a better human than I could have possibly imagined.

No book can be its best without an editor. David, you have helped me make six piles of words into books now. And no writer can be their best without an agent. Jenn, you keep me from the brink and make it happen. Let's keep doing it, team! Along with truckloads of appreciation for Maeve, Sophie, and the production team, as well as the host of marketing, publicity, and sales fairies that get my books into readers' hands. Becca is BFFs with all of you.

Librarians and educators—you are doing amazing work in the face of nonsense. Overflowing gratitude for your dedication to getting quality, inclusive literature into every kid's hands.

And _____ (write your name here). Thanks for reading.

ABOUT THE AUTHOR

Alex Gino is now the author of six queer and progressive middle grade novels, including the Stonewall- and Lambda Award–winning *Melissa*. They love glitter, ice cream, gardening, wordplay, and stories that reflect the complexity of being alive, and they would take a quiet coffee date with a friend over a loud and crowded party any day. Alex grew up on Staten Island, NY, where they started telling stories before they could hold a pencil. They now happily live, along with Thunder the Wonder Cat, in a tiny town in Western Massachusetts that *does* have a stop sign at its main intersection. They have lots of great friends, both real and otherwise.